"I WANTED TO KNOW IF THIS AFTERNOON WAS A dream," he murmured.

"Which part?"

"Us together. On a bed."

"You fell," she said quickly.

"You stayed."

"You were worn out."

"Not too worn out to know I had a woman under me."

She shrugged as if it didn't matter. Her shoulder grazed his. "An automatic physical response," she said. "I didn't take it seriously."

"We're any man and woman, is that it?"

"Could be."

He kissed her again, proving her all wrong.

WHAT ARE *LOVESWEPT* ROMANCES?

They are stories of true romance and touching emotion. We believe those two very important ingredients are constants in our highly sensual and very believable stories in the LOVESWEPT line. Our goal is to give you, the reader, stories of consistently high quality that may sometimes make you laugh, sometimes make you cry, but are always fresh and creative and contain many delightful surprises within their pages.

Most romance fans read an enormous number of books. Those they truly love, they keep. Others may be traded with friends and soon forgotten. We hope that each LOVE-SWEPT romance will be a treasure—a "keeper." We will always try to publish

LOVE STORIES YOU'LL NEVER FORGET
BY AUTHORS YOU'LL ALWAYS REMEMBER

The Editors

Loveswept ®788

FUGITIVE
FATHER

TERRY LAWRENCE

BANTAM BOOKS
NEW YORK · TORONTO · LONDON · SYDNEY · AUCKLAND

FUGITIVE FATHER

A Bantam Book / May 1996

ISBN 0-553-44493-X

Published simultaneously in the United States and Canada

Bantam Books are published by Bantam Books, a division of Bantam Dou-
bleday Dell Publishing Group, Inc. Its trademark, consisting of the words
"Bantam Books" and the portrayal of a rooster, is Registered in U.S.
Patent and Trademark Office and in other countries. Marca Registrada.
Bantam Books, 1540 Broadway, New York, New York 10036.

PRINTED IN THE UNITED STATES OF AMERICA

OPM   0 9 8 7 6 5 4 3 2 1

ONE

"We'll leave a light on for you." Ben grunted. His thigh hurt like a son of a bitch and no amount of gallows humor could dissolve the stony pit of fear in his stomach. He leaned against a tree, fighting wooziness and wishful thinking. Someone had left a light burning in a cottage on the cliff edge overlooking the rocky Lake Superior shore. A blurry figure walked past the window. A woman.

He didn't ask how he knew. He'd guessed wrong a lot lately—and paid for it in blood. It could've been a branch swaying, a trick of lightning. Thunder cracked then rolled, ricocheting off the rain-blackened tree trunks. He'd been heading for the shore; he'd never expected civilization.

Wiping rain, sweat, and a sticky smear off his forehead, he asked himself the hard questions first. This was the only house for miles; what if she was in league with the men who'd shot him? What if they were inside already?

He'd find out soon enough.

Or bleed to death waiting.

He gave the tourniquet a twist, bracing himself for the hot streak of pain. A searing ache pulsed through him like the afterimage of a flashbulb—or the flash of a gun fired in the dark.

It seemed like hours ago. He'd been watching from cover. He'd counted four men, a dozen crates. He'd completely missed the lookout patrolling the perimeter of the deserted logging camp. A smuggler's paradise, the Lake Superior shore. Most of it was isolated wilderness with miles of uninhabited coastline. Remote. What was that saying? "This isn't the end of the world, but you can see it from here."

He'd spoken out loud. Another brain-fogged mistake. This would be the end of *his* world if he didn't get moving. His legs felt like lead—one from a bullet and the other from carrying his weight. He'd run, staggered, and a couple of times just plain crawled through the undergrowth, hoping the roar of their all-terrain vehicles and the punishing storm would drown out the crackle of dead leaves, downed branches, and his jagged breathing.

They'd put up quite a search. He granted them that much. His pursuers didn't lack for nerve. Crossing Lake Superior in anything less than a freighter took guts. How they transported their cache overland was the big question. In such a sparsely populated area, they either kept very quiet or a lot of local people joined in.

Like the woman in the house? He turned to get a better look at the light. A snapping twig stopped him cold. The end of the world crept closer.

His mind raced. He had no weapon—he'd lost it in the woods. What strength he possessed seeped out a gash in his thigh. But if that was an innocent civilian in there, he had to stop whoever lurked behind him. If gunshots lured her outside, his followers might "clean up" any witnesses.

He pressed his back to the tree trunk, automatically placing himself between the house and them. "So what're you gonna do, hotshot? Stare them down?"

He looked at the light one more time. An odd longing knotted in his chest like a fist. Before he staggered off to lay down a false trail, possibly to die in the middle of nowhere, he wanted to make damn sure he wasn't doing it for an automatic timer.

She walked by again. A woman, apparently alone, dark hair to her shoulders. The flicker of a fireplace bathed her in gold. He would've liked to know her name.

He shut his eyes tight and waited for another crackle. The drumming rain died to a misty whisper. The lake rasped against the stony shore. An owl hooted. Something scurried by, something rodent-sized. God gave him a break; the clouds parted. He used the slash of moonlight to scan the trees. No movement. No shadows that didn't belong there. Maybe they'd given up. Maybe he'd been given one more chance.

He hopped away from the tree, arm outstretched for balance. Pine resin stuck to his shirt. Branches clasped him like a woman reluctant to let go. He must be losing it. No woman had ever held on to him that way. Not even Carla.

He mentally mapped out which trees he'd use for support between where he was and the front door. One light burned in a downstairs window. A woman waited. It was all he needed.

❖━━━━━❖

The huge brass knocker boomed the length of the entrance hall. Bridget jumped out of her leather chair. She'd have jumped out of her skin if it hadn't been attached.

"Bridget Bethany Bernard!" Quoting her mother's favorite oath failed to calm her hammering heart.

Listening intently, she stepped out of the fireplace's cozy aura and waited for another knock. When a minute stretched by, she inched up the three pine stairs leading from the great room into the hall. A log snapped on the fire. She whirled, poker raised. She hadn't even realized she'd grabbed it.

"I told you not to read *The Shining*," she whispered. No sensible woman, having agreed to stay in a huge deserted lodge for six months alone, would dare read Stephen King.

She'd laid in a supply. "Guess you could always throw a book at them." She waited in vain for another knock. "Maybe it was a bear."

"A bear using a knocker? Smart bear," she retorted.

Legs trembling, mind repeating the low northern crime statistics, she slid her slippered feet along the gleaming wood floor. The entrance hall stretched thirty feet and towered eighteen. Rafter beams of rough-hewn oak arched overhead, cathedral-style. Sound carried, echoed, and was amplified. Light died. The gloom deepened as she neared the massive split-log door. From fifteen feet away she discerned the iron latch thrown securely across it.

Emboldened by the certainty no one could force

his or her way in, she leaned into the door, fingers splayed on the cold iron hinges. The knocker boomed.

She jumped a mile. Roundly cursing herself and whoever the fool was scaring the living daylights out of her, she pushed every old-fashioned pearl-tipped light button on the panel. Two deer-antler chandeliers lit the length of the hall. The parlors on both sides came alive with light. The front porch should have been bathed in it.

No one had thought to cut a window in the door. She made a note. Then she listened to the silence. There was no scurrying of startled animals, no giggling teenagers, nothing but the uncanny sense of someone on the other side, listening, breathing, waiting. . . .

She cleared her throat. "Who's there?"

"I need help."

Bridget considered the low male voice. It was resigned, rough, a touch frustrated. If a person really was in trouble . . . ? She'd be wise not to open the door.

All the same, they were miles from anything but dense woods. If he really needed help . . . ? She gripped the poker in her right hand, lifted the foot-long iron latch, turned the handle, and jumped back. When nothing happened, she leaned forward. The heavy door swung silently open.

He didn't move. Her first impression summed up the basics: average height, solid build, dark hair, around thirty. And tired, life-tired. He pressed his shoulder against the jamb as if he'd been leaning there for hours. Not false friendly—genuinely exhausted. Even his hair looked weary, lank with rain and sweat. A bloody streak on his forehead underlined a welt possibly inflicted by a tree branch. "Thanks for opening the door."

She stared at him in shock. "How far did you hike?"

He mutely accepted her scolding, then squinted at her under furrowed brows. He looked convinced that what he was about to say would not be well received. "You aren't one of those women who faint at the sight of blood, are you?"

She stepped back smartly, letting him get a good look at the poker. Tearing her gaze from his tense expression, she raked him from head to toe.

Beneath the grime, his hair was black, arrow straight, parted more or less down the middle. Chiseled cheekbones, deep skin tones, and a Superman jaw gave him a stark ethnic look. He could have been Native American, Mexican, Italian, or Greek. He'd fit in in a lot of places. All of them dangerous.

He put a lot of effort into softening his look. But the reassuring smile didn't do diddly to erase the pain collected at the corners of his mouth. "I'm harmless, really."

And she was Eleanor Roosevelt.

His shirt was a dirty plaid, standard fare up north if one discounted the rips and the mud. Cuffs rolled to his elbows revealed solid forearms laced with more scrapes. His pants were olive-green khaki.

"Don't fall apart on me here." He righted himself, using the jamb for support.

She pointed the poker like a sword.

"I won't hurt you."

"I know you won't." She bobbed the poker tip for emphasis, pointing at the tourniquet on his thigh. "Was that bandanna always that color?"

Black and dripping with blood? He didn't bother looking. His eyes stayed on hers. There was no twinkle, no sparkle in them, just a silent plea for her help. "I got shot," he said flatly.

She waited.

He shifted on his good leg, doing his damnedest to turn a wince into a smile. "Hunting accident. Dropped my gun. Stupid really. Lost the way back. Been following the shoreline. Just call it the camping trip from hell." He ran a hand through his hair. A black lock fell across his forehead. His shrug said "trust me." He was charming, a little careless maybe—

And she didn't believe a word of it.

"If I had a good leg, I'd be kicking myself with it." He chuckled, pressing the wound as unobtrusively as he could. Fresh blood seeped between his fingers.

Bridget gripped the poker.

"I think it's a deep graze," he continued, trying to get her attention back on his face. "All this moving around made it bleed a lot worse than it is."

"And what makes you an expert?"

"It's my blood."

Their gazes met. Suddenly she knew what it was about him that struck her as familiar. Those eyes. Playing polite was a luxury he couldn't afford much longer. She recognized that cut-to-the-chase urgency. It was lay-it-on-the-line time, the look a man got when he stared death in the face and found one more sliver of life to hold on to. She thought she'd left that look in San Francisco. With Richie.

His shudder gave her the impression he'd been trying not to let the cold win. Rain and mud molded his clothes to him like second skin. By all rights he should be freezing. Any man trying to gain her sympathy would be pouring on the suffering.

He held his in check, jaw clenched, cheekbones sharply outlined. He glanced down at his bloody fingers, measuring how much he'd lost, how much time he had. A stray lock of hair tumbled across his forehead.

She tightened her grip.

He sighed as if painfully aware he was getting nowhere. Taking a breath halfway into his lungs, he stopped sharply. "Look, I know you have no reason to let me in. You should never let a man into your house at night. Especially when you're alone."

"Who says I'm letting you in?" She took another step back. "And who says I'm alone?"

"Try that." The lock of hair swayed.

She glanced in the direction he nodded. An antique gun was mounted on the wall at the foot of the staircase. She doubted it was loaded. Even if it was, it was probably so filled with dust and grime, it'd blow up in her hands if she fired it. "Okay, I will!"

She edged backward up the stairs and pried the gun from its rack. Poker in her left hand, gun in her right, she waved him inside.

It took him a minute. He gathered all his strength to take the one measly step across the threshold.

She felt ridiculous and cruel. She stayed where she was. "Sorry about the paranoia."

"Hey, you have no reason to trust me."

"For a psycho-killer you're not very good at worming your way into a woman's confidence."

He was inside, wasn't he? Ben studied the uneven lengths of oak and inlaid cherrywood at his feet. He took one step and nearly pitched forward on his face.

Staggering to his left, he collapsed against the hall table. The wooden legs screeched. The poker clattered down the stairs.

She rushed to his side. "You really are hurt."

"Or else I'm a damn good actor. You shouldn't be fooled by a little—"

She set the gun on the table. "You need help!"

"And you need lessons in self-defense! *Never* put your gun down!"

She gaped at him.

What the hell was he doing yelling at her? The anger was strictly for him. No matter how tangled that forest, he should have never lost his gun. What would he protect her with if the smugglers came after him? He hated being helpless. Worse, he hated anyone being in danger because of him. That's why he worked solo. Always.

He ran a hand over his face, marking time until he had to look at her. So much for acting harmless. She'd be frightened of him now, wary.

He slanted her a glance. Unafraid and unimpressed, she coolly surveyed the damage. "Tell me one thing. If I pointed a gun at you, could you walk ten feet?"

He doubted it.

"I figured that much. You may not be harmless, but you're definitely disabled. Here, put your arm around my shoulders." She tossed her hair back and scooped it over her right shoulder. Lifting his elbow, she wedged herself under his armpit. "Work with me here."

He tried. Right side hugged to her, he let his arm curve over her narrow shoulders. She fit her left arm around his waist. "Let's try a step."

He looked at the parlor opposite the table. The walls were logs, rustic, hand-hewn, but not the furniture. White sofas lined an off-white carpet with an Indian design. White slipcovered chairs sat next to tables covered with soft pink fringed doilies. "Not in there."

"Then where?"

He hated to say it, but there was no way he'd stay on the ground floor and risk people spotting him through the windows the way he'd spotted her. "Up there."

She didn't dignify that with an upward glance. "Right. And you're going to collapse ten steps up. Or will you wait until we're halfway?"

"What you lack in bedside manner you make up for in sarcasm. Anyone ever tell you that?"

"Only everyone. It put a real dent in the old nursing career. Let's try the great room, then. There's a fire, it's warm—"

"I need a bathroom. Hot water. Soap and towels."

Measuring the length of the hall, she sighed. "You may have a point. The kitchen is at the end of the west wing, down there and to the left. The bedrooms are probably closer." She glanced up as if imploring a higher power for strength. "We're replacing every mattress upstairs, so I guess you can bleed on one of 'em. Just promise me you'll hold up until we get there."

"I promise."

One step. Two. Each one was a battle while they coordinated their movements.

"What's your name?" she asked.

"Ben." He hoped the fight for balance covered his hesitation.

"Hi, Ben."

She had to have a name too. For the moment the next step took all his concentration. After the fourth he wondered if blood loss had affected his judgment. Outside, he'd used trees as crutches. This woman was five-foot-nothing, if that, and no more than a hundred pounds. Twelve stairs and a landing loomed above them. He tried to take on more of the weight.

Feeling him lean away, she adjusted her grip higher on his waist. The cry escaped before he could stop it.

She gasped. "Did that hurt?"

He gritted his teeth until the pain passed. "I think I broke a rib." He panted, sweat breaking out freely on his brow. "Give me a minute."

She gave him plenty. It took most of that time for him to realize she wasn't pausing out of sympathy. When he looked over, suspicion darkened her big brown eyes.

"What's wrong?"

"Nothing." Chirpy, fake, the woman had no future as a liar. She hustled him up another step. Resting on the next, she tried casual conversation. "So. How do you break a rib dropping a gun?"

A loaded question if he ever heard one. "I fell, after the bullet hit me. Must have landed on a log. Or a rock. What did you say your name was?"

"I didn't. It's Bridget."

"Bridget." Another stair. "You don't have to believe me."

"Another valiant attempt to win my confidence."

He stopped, swaying slightly. "I mean it. If you think I'm dangerous, you don't feel safe—just grab that rib again."

"Deliberately?"

"A man comes into your house, if he does something you don't like, you let him have it."

"You sound like my dad. Are you talking me *into* this or *out* of it?"

Into it, apparently. She gripped him lower around the hip and got them up one more stair. Perspiration glowed on her forehead. She blew a breath at her wispy bangs.

The next time they rested, he reached over, skimming the hair off her brow with his fingertip. "Better?"

She stared up at him, her lips parted in surprise. Breath barely issued between them. His gentleness had surprised her. The subtle flush of color in her cheeks surprised *him*.

She was beautiful. He'd noticed that from the first. In the chandelier light her skin was porcelain fine. He figured her age near thirty, more from the experience in her eyes than from any lines around them. She had the patrician features of a woman who'd be beautiful at sixty. But big? Never. She was frail as fine china— but strong in ways that counted.

And yet, ever since their eyes met, she'd been frozen in place, waiting for something from him. If they'd been in any other situation, he'd have taken it as a signal, a sensual reaction between a man and a woman. He'd have kissed her.

He stayed where he was. What he knew about women had gotten him divorced and alone for the last seven years. He'd dedicated his life to his job. Tonight that life depended on her.

He brushed at her bangs, a gruff friendly gesture.

He rubbed the muddy pads of his fingers together. "Got you dirty. Sorry."

Flustered, her gaze scoured the next stair tread for a foothold. "Let's get you to bed. Then we'll worry about cleaning up."

The phrase struck a nerve. Ben glanced uneasily over his shoulder. The door gaped open behind them. He'd been distracted—dangerously so. His pursuers could still be out there.

"It'd be easier if you paid attention," she scolded.

Outside, a flash of light illuminated the porch. Lightning? Headlights? He didn't want to make her any more suspicious. Nevertheless— "That door," he rasped out. "Aren't you afraid it'll rain in?"

"I'm a little busy right now. Whew! Let's rest on the landing, then four more stairs."

"Maybe you should bolt it."

She leaned against the railing, hands outstretched. The damp fabric of her loose jersey clung, matting against her chest wherever she held him. Out of breath, she smiled and glanced at the door. "Afraid of bears?"

He flattened himself to the log wall, letting it take his weight. "Bridget, lock it. The latch would be a good idea too."

Her deep breaths slowed to a shallow rise and fall. Emotions flickered through her eyes—humor, disbelief, suspicion, a glimmer of fear. He didn't like the fear. All the same, a healthy dose might keep them both alive. "Close it, Bridget. Then lock it."

She edged off the landing, her gaze glued to his, and picked her way down the steps. Halfway down she broke into a run. Slamming the door, she doused the porch lights and the two parlors. The iron latch clanged into place.

Releasing the deepest breath he could manage, Ben closed his eyes. He rested his head against a bumpy log. At last he was safe.

The unmistakable click of a cocked gun opened his eyes.

TWO

"Who are you?" She'd wrapped both hands around the antique wooden stock. One index finger hovered on the guard, the other twitched on the trigger. "Who are you?" she demanded.

"My name's Ben." That much was true.

"What are you doing here?"

"Bleeding on your floor."

"What are you doing here?"

"Hunting." He didn't specify what or whom.

"I'm serious." To prove it, she cocked the gun again.

He was about to tell her you couldn't cock an already cocked gun when her thumb slipped and the hammer slammed forward. The empty click echoed up and down the hall.

"I didn't think that was loaded," he said dryly.

Her explicit curse surprised him. She slapped the gun onto the step and clambered level with him. "I knew damn well it wasn't! Now what am I going to do with you?"

"Help me upstairs."

"I'll hit you in the thigh if you try anything."

He gravely regarded her wagging finger. "Honey, you could knock me over with a feather."

"Don't play cute."

"Who me?" He felt downright giddy. Either she was getting taller or he was sliding down the wall. He couldn't be hurt *that* bad. A small voice reminded him shock could kill even a moderately injured person. All the same, he let his eyes drift shut and his head sag. The steps could wait. She could bring the bandages down here. And aspirin. He had this killer headache. . . .

She slapped him. "Don't you die on me. You stay conscious."

"I'm trying."

"I'm calling an ambulance."

"No!" He gripped her wrist. There was no better way to lead his pursuers to her door than with flashing lights and sirens. "I can make it. I just need your help. Talk to me."

"About camping trips?"

"I don't want to go into shock." That made her listen. He looked her straight in the eye. "I'm scared."

That made her move. She helped him up. "Four more stairs. Think you can make it?"

He figured she'd underestimated the distance by at least two. He let it pass. What were a few white lies between friends?

Shuffling into the first bedroom with an attached bath, Bridget toppled him onto the bed. She linked her fingers beneath his left calf and lifted his wounded leg onto the bed. "Comfortable?"

"Warm."

She frowned. "I don't like one-word answers. We're supposed to keep you talking, remember? I'll get extra blankets."

"Yeah."

"And some hot water. We'll need towels, washcloths, the first-aid kit, bandages."

Rattling off a list of things to do, she made an internal list of things she *didn't* know. She didn't know first aid for bullet wounds. She didn't know if the stair climb or the pain had brought out the sweat on his brow. She knew the wet clothes had to come off. She had to warm him up. She had to stem the bleeding until the ambulance got there. She had to find some gloves.

He lay on the bed staring at the ceiling. A vein beat in his pain-clenched jaw. His eyes focused on the light fixture overhead.

"Ben? Ben!"

"I'm here."

"I'll be right back. Don't you die on me."

"I'm fine." His gaze shifted from the ceiling to her. A smile fought through his squint. "I'm alive anyway."

"And I'm either a fool or the world's busiest Good Samaritan."

Minutes later Bridget stood outside the closed bedroom door catching her breath. She'd raced downstairs, found two dusty first-aid kits in the butler's pantry, then ran from one partly redecorated room to another looking for paint supplies. The old kits didn't take AIDS into consideration; plastic painter's gloves would have to do.

Not that coming in contact with blood was her major concern. His hunting story wouldn't fool Pollyanna. His injuries were real, but who knew what strength he held in reserve? She still felt the well-muscled body she'd helped up those stairs. What if he turned on her?

What did it matter?

The quiet voice of her conscience made her pause. She could wallow in paranoia all she wanted. The fact of the matter was the man needed help. She'd seen it in his eyes. He was scared and hurt. How he got that way wasn't her business to judge. Her brother had taught her that lesson.

She would bathe Ben's wounds and do what she could in the bandaging department. When he was safely asleep she'd sneak downstairs to call an ambulance. She could have called one on this trip, but his woozy replies put his care first on her list.

She opened the door and peeked inside. "Still alive?"

"Working on it."

She strode to the antique washbasin beside the bed, refusing to let the sight of his chest stall her halfway across the room. He'd managed to unbutton his shirt. It lay open to his waist, revealing a tanned expanse of skin crisscrossed with black hair and pink scratches. They reminded Bridget of the damage inflicted by a woman's nails. Her eyes met his.

"What are you waiting for?" His low voice sent a chill down her spine.

She set the red-and-white kits on a chair and

picked up the pitcher. "I'll be in the bathroom getting hot water. We may have to cut up some dust cloths for bandages." She backed into the bathroom. Her back bounced off the jamb. "I'll be back."

"I'm not going anywhere."

Her laugh emerged as rusty as the water. She ran both taps full blast until the water turned crystal clear and ice-cold. "Getting hot water to the second floor takes forever," she called over the clattering pipes.

Getting her mind off Ben's body took longer. She had no business rating his physique. She'd seen plenty of good-looking bodies in her day. She could have treated his as nothing but flesh, and would have, if it hadn't been for that look, the one on the stairs that had stolen her breath, her composure, her precious hard-won solitude.

Something had happened. A spark. A link. Her chest felt heavy and empty at once. When she gave in to it her skin tingled and her cheeks flamed. She hoped to heaven he hadn't noticed. She'd come there to start anew and alone. Life didn't hand a woman anything—much less deliver it to her door.

She put her hand under the faucet, accidentally spraying the mirror with droplets. "I should have never given up cigarettes."

"What?"

"Everything's going to be fine," she announced cheerfully. "We'll get you cleaned up and warmed up, and if you're good, I may even make you some chicken soup."

"Huh."

She scrubbed her hands as thoroughly as a doctor entering surgery. By the time she was done, the water had turned lukewarm. She ran a wet hand through her hair and caught a glimpse of herself in the mirror.

Her shoulder-length hair was tangled and flat. Her loose-fitting blue jersey hung lifelessly on her body. The material adhered to her, a large damp patch darkening her side. Two tiny half-moon shadows underlined her peaked nipples. Separating the material from her skin, she pushed up the long sleeves and glanced down at her stretch pants and slippers. There was nothing remotely sexy about her attire. This early in the summer her ankles were bony and pasty white. Any shivers of attraction were one-sided and entirely her imagination. "Hormones and nicotine withdrawal."

So why was she hiding in the bathroom?

Steam rose from the sink. She'd never been so happy to be in hot water. Throwing open the linen closet, she filled her arms with towels, hugging them to her chest. "Time to get you undressed," she called. Tossing her reflection a you-be-careful look, she marched into his room.

Pulling up a chair, she set the pitcher of hot water on a second cane-seated antique and plumped the towels beside it. "How's the leg?"

"Throbbing. Less bleeding."

"Then let's start at the top and work our way down." She put her hand under his neck, wedging her forearm under his shoulder blades. "I need you to sit up."

He braced himself. His abdomen tightened and muscles rippled across his chest. Working together they got him half sitting, half leaning against the headboard.

"Can you stay there?"

He nodded tightly.

His body *was* beautiful. Objectively speaking, he was in peak condition. He was also ice-cold and in more pain than he wanted her to know.

She worked quickly, peeling the shirt off his shoulders. She stuffed pillows behind his back for support. The wet shirt hit the ground with a slap. She briskly rubbed a towel across his clammy skin. Wringing out a washcloth, she tugged on the wrinkled gloves and perched on the bed. Leaning close, she dabbed his face. When she attacked the welt on his forehead he wrested his chin away. "Hold still. You're worse than a little kid."

"No one's confused me with a kid in a long time."

No kidding. His gravelly voice was as suggestive as wineglasses before a fireplace. Rasping words through those clenched teeth couldn't be easy. Sure as shootin' it shouldn't be sexy.

"There!" She sat back.

The bed sagged. He hissed in pain and reached for his thigh.

She scooted off the bed. "I'm sorry."

"It's nothing."

"Maybe I should look at that."

He found the used towel and bunched it against his thigh. "Do the chest."

"Think so?"

His gaze rested on hers a fraction of a second too long. "I think it'd be easier on both of us."

Unwarranted heat flushed her cheeks again. He couldn't mean this was affecting him too. Surely she was reading into things.

"A side of ribs it is," she declared. Clutching a roll of gauze bandages, she blinked in dismay when it bounded out of her hand and unrolled across the floor.

She got off the bed and reached. Each time her fingers grasped for it it rolled another three feet. "Did I warn you you were being tended by the world's greatest klutz?" Another reach. Another three feet. "Excuse me." She crawled under the bed. Object in hand, she was left with the unlovely prospect of wriggling backward toward the light, her rear end high in the air. Graceful it was not. "Bet this never happens to Mother Teresa."

She assumed his grunt substituted for a laugh. Standing, she held out the unfurled bandage. Dust bunnies stuck to it as if it were flypaper. "Ruined."

"You can use it. It isn't an open wound."

She glowered doubtfully at his chest. The deep bruise beneath his left nipple obviously needed attention. "Are you sure it's broken?"

"Feel it."

That hadn't been her intent. His tone brooked no argument. He had natural authority, this Ben did. He became more daunting by the moment.

She sat gingerly on the bed, her fingers splaying gently across his ribs. Inching her way toward the broken one, she felt him catch his breath. "Sorry."

"You'll never tell that way."

"I don't want to hurt you."

He roughly covered her hand with his, pressing their fingers together the length of the rib. It was Bridget's turn to hold her breath.

After a long moment he released a shuddering one. "It's in one piece. If it's fractured, the bandages will keep it from breaking off completely. Don't want any jagged edges. Bridget?"

She'd gone totally pale. "What are you, some kind of marine?"

He laughed, banged his head against the headboard when he felt the consequences, and clutched a handful of mattress until the pain passed. Fresh sweat popped out on his upper lip. She must have looked worried. He smiled for her sake. "I'm not that tough."

"Right. And this bed isn't made of iron."

His face was inches from hers. Her lips were soft pink, pale and naked. Small dents from her even white teeth marked her lower lip.

He'd watched her ever since that awkward moment when she'd complimented him on how tough he was. In pain, he'd gripped what he thought was the mattress, only to find the warmth of her thigh beneath his palm. She'd pretended it hadn't happened. He'd ordered her to bind his ribs tighter.

She'd obeyed. Her breasts skimmed his chest through her jersey every time she reached around his back for the roll of bandages. Her top drooped off her left shoulder, revealing her collarbone and the soft white mound of a shoulder. She'd impatiently pulled her hair to one side. Its fragrance teased him whenever she bent close.

He craned his neck, surreptitiously skimming his cheek across that sumptuous midnight. A few strands caught on his stubbled cheek. She smelled like an angel. He smelled like hell.

Finished, she corkscrewed around to reach the scissors. Covering her hand in his, he held the bandage in place while she tied the knot. Satisfied, she looked up.

There they were, inches apart. And there they stayed, so close, all they had to do was kiss.

She pulled back.

Whatever was going on in those troubled eyes, he'd better ease it. She had no business trusting him. That didn't mean he wouldn't use her trust to his advantage. He tried a breath. "Feels better already. You make a good nurse."

"Strictly a hobby."

He lowered his voice suggestively. "Do it often?"

She paused as if she'd heard a snake rattle.

Dumb move. He'd meant it as a joke, a double entendre intended to turn fleeting sexual awareness into harmless flirtation.

Instead her eyes turned very calm, her expression guarded. "My brother has AIDS. I just spent two months nursing him through pneumonia."

He swallowed a curse at his own expense. "I'm sorry." Words seemed inadequate. So did the sorry gesture of patting her on the arm.

She moved out of reach, sorting through the first-aid kit, taking stock of what they'd need next. She'd averted her face, bracing herself for anything he might dish out: scorn, suspicion, prejudice.

Ben would sooner break another rib than prove her right. He stuck with the obvious. "How'd he get it?"

"You mean did he deserve it?"

"I mean there are a lot of ways—" He hardly knew the woman, and she had him on the defensive faster than a sumo wrestler could toss him on a mat. "I didn't mean—"

"He's gay. He and his lover thought they were

playing it safe." She tucked a foot under her and swept her hair off her face. "Okay?"

Ben didn't know what he was supposed to say. He'd never understood the lifestyle. That didn't mean he liked the idea of people dying young.

She scanned his face, seeing straight through the mask of reserved judgment. "You should be grateful. If it weren't for him, you wouldn't be getting my help now."

"You learned nursing to help him?"

"I learned sweet-nothing-at-all about bullet wounds in San Francisco. What I learned was that it doesn't matter how foolish people are or how risky their behavior—when they're sick they're sick. They need help. I did a lot of that out there. For Richie and some of his friends. You benefit. Ironic, huh?"

He stilled the hand plucking reluctantly at the beginning of the bandage roll. "I'm sorry."

She looked up, more dignified and more achingly vulnerable than she realized. "Yeah, maybe you are."

Her forgiving smile nearly broke his heart. "How old was he?"

Her brows rose. A smile curved her soft lips. "He's twenty-nine, two years younger than me, fighting cancer but otherwise doing fine."

"I thought you said you'd nursed him—"

"Until he sent me away. Turns out his friends know more about caring for AIDS patients than I ever will. Unfortunately. Richie told me to go home. 'To live.'"

Ben knew nothing of her family or her past. He knew a brave front when he saw one, a shrug trying too hard to be upbeat.

"He said I was living for two now. 'Live life to the

fullest,' that's the game plan. I'm supposed to stop waiting."

"For what?"

"For life to happen. For things to come along. Whatever I want, I'm to go out and get it."

"Meaning what? Money, career?"

"Meaning none of this is helping your leg."

It was his fault. He'd been quietly adjusting his posture. Muscles he hadn't known he had clamored to make his acquaintance.

She got back to business, peeling the cloth away from his leg to get a look at the bleeding. Something had passed between them, somehow ice had broken. She slapped him on the opposite thigh, a grin on her face. "What say we get those pants off, sailor?"

"Is that what we've been postponing?"

"Maybe I wanted you to know I've seen a lot of male bodies. Some of them even better than yours."

"I bet."

She unbuckled his belt buckle. "Problem is, not a one of them was interested in me."

"You didn't tell me they were blind too."

She folded his belt back. "Thanks for the compliment."

"Anytime."

She unhooked the top button. "Don't worry. No man's at his best in cold wet underwear."

"Thanks for understanding."

She grinned. The zipper slid down. It didn't hurt. He stiffened all the same. She parted the fabric. "I guessed right. A boxer man."

"Don't look too close. I've got a reputation to maintain."

"A good-looker like you? I wouldn't be surprised."

She wrestled the clinging fabric from one side to the other and got it halfway down his hips. "I think you're going to have to move for me, Ben."

"Most women don't have to tell me."

"Very funny." It was working, Bridget thought. The playful flirtation, the easy banter. As long as she treated him like a patient and a friend, they'd be fine.

Then he put his hand over hers, trapping her palm against the clammy cotton boxers. Her heart skittered. "What is it?"

"Before we go any further—"

"Yes?"

"I'm going to have to untie that."

She glanced down. The tourniquet lay heavy with blood against his leg. "Shouldn't I—"

"It'd be easier for me."

She understood. He needed to keep the sudden easing of pressure under his control; it was the only way to manage the pain. Balancing on his right elbow, he reached for the short stick he'd twisted into the tourniquet. Unwinding it, he gritted his teeth in advance. All the time he never took his eyes off her.

It was as if he drew his strength from her presence, her endurance. For his sake, she couldn't falter. She remembered that, the elemental human need to have someone nearby, for people to know they weren't suffering alone. It was an unearned trust she'd been granted a dozen times. She'd do anything to deserve it.

He bit off a pain-filled breath. She clamped her hands in her lap.

His croaking laugh startled her. "You should see your face. You look worse than me."

"Don't bet on it. Is there anything I can do besides have sympathy pains?"

He shook his head. Locks of hair fell on his cheeks from both sides. Sweat chilled him like dew. "It'll just have to hurt."

She bit her lip.

The wet fabric was being difficult, the knot dense and slippery. "Ever see the part in *Gone With the Wind* where they saw the guy's leg off?"

She gave him an unamused glare. "I'll get the carving knife."

Another husky chuckle. "I'm just saying it could be worse."

"I don't see how."

The stick fell from the bandanna. Ben plucked out the remaining knot and threw the whole soggy mess off the bed. Exhausted, he lay back. "Your turn."

If he expected her to laugh, she'd have to breathe again first. Blood flowed freely but less than she'd feared. She folded a washcloth. "Press this on it until I can get the bandage ready."

"Your hands aren't even shaking."

"Just you wait. When I leave this room I'll turn into a noodle." She tugged his pants to his knees and left them there. Right then the gash commanded her full attention.

He turned his head on the pillow. "Got any alcohol in your magic kit?"

"If you think I'm pouring pure alcohol on an open wound—"

"I promise I won't scream."

"No."

"It may need it."

"It may need stitches."

"Then get me a needle and thread."

Blood drained from her face. She felt green. "I've seen enough macho demonstrations for one night."

"Then tell me how it looks."

She peered at the wound. "Deep. Ugly. Nonfatal. I hope. It looks like the bullet cut a channel across your thigh and went on its merry way."

"Embedded in some rotting tree trunk, I hope. Bridget."

She paused, arrested by the weight of his hand on her arm. Her gaze stayed glued to it. Every inch of her felt his unwavering scrutiny as if it were a rough caress.

"Give me a cloth with some alcohol on it."

"Can't it wait?"

"Until when? Until it's infected? Until it turns to blood poisoning?" His fingers gripped tighter, claws circling her wrist. "Or are you waiting until they get here?"

"Who?"

If she was on the bad guy's side, the woman was going to have to do something about that face. Emotions flitted across it faster than a purse snatcher on the run.

Her shoulders squared. Her voice got higher. She looked guilty as hell. "Until who gets here?"

"The people you called."

"I didn't call anyone."

"Then whoever you were going to call."

He watched her consider a lie, then give it up. "You need an ambulance."

"All I need is that alcohol."

Lips tight, she poured a healthy shot on a washcloth and handed him the rest of the bottle. "You do it. I'll be in the bathroom throwing up."

He still wasn't sure he trusted her.

"I won't call anyone unless the bleeding gets worse," she promised, nodding at the bottle as an afterthought. "Or unless you pass out."

Seeing as he didn't have much say in it, he agreed. "Deal."

THREE

She rested her hand on the telephone. Sitting in the log kitchen, she stared at the copper pots hanging from the beams. Pewabic tiles lined the granite counters, their watery blue glaze reminiscent of the lake whispering outside. A pine table stretched before her, bare except for a telephone. She noted the absence of the ashtray she'd have automatically set beside it.

Her fingernails tick-tocked on the old black telephone. The clock said twelve-fifteen. She'd promised him she wouldn't call.

Neither one of them was doing real well in the truth department.

Craving a cigarette, she paced to the humming refrigerator and found a carrot to munch. She'd left him sleeping fitfully. Resting her cheek against the refrigerator's cool door, she remembered the rest of their evening.

When he'd finished cleansing the wound, he'd called her name. She'd peeled her forehead from the bathroom mirror and gone back into the room. It had smelled of raw alcohol and male sweat.

"The patient's still alive," he'd joked.

"The nurse isn't doing too well."

"I think she's doing just fine."

She'd tried not to let the compliment get to her. His courage had already impressed her beyond measure. So had his consideration. He'd not only saved her the sight of his enduring something she could barely watch, he'd saved her the embarrassment of removing those boxers. A tense, tanned hand had clutched the bedspread over his midsection. Bare legs stuck out beneath it.

She'd bent to collect the pile of wet clothes he'd flung on the floor.

"You don't have to wash them. Just let 'em dry."

"I was thinking of throwing them away."

"I have to wear something."

"I'll get you replacements."

"Where?"

"Pick a room. This lodge was more or less abandoned in the twenties. There are closets full of old clothes. Suits, suspenders, spats, sock garters—"

That's when she'd realized what she was staring at wasn't a sock garter.

His features had hardened. "It's an ankle holster."

"I know that."

Sitting in the kitchen an hour later, her mouth went dry all over again. She gripped the receiver. She'd known he was lying about hunting. There was no reason the sight of that holster should make her skin crawl.

He'd remained deathly still. "Bridget."

She'd picked up speed, flinging up the dust ruffle

to see if there were any stray bits of clothing or snippets of bandages to toss.

"Bridget."

"Important to get the drop on those moose, isn't it?"

"The gun's gone."

"What were you hunting?"

His face was flint, his voice stone. "Whatever's in season."

"And that would be?"

"We'll talk about the one that got away in the morning."

If there was a morning. She'd intended to get him out of there as soon as she locked him in, sneaked downstairs, and called an ambulance—and maybe the police for good measure.

That had been the plan. As she crunched another carrot her resolve faltered. She picked up the receiver. It was nine-thirty San Francisco time. She stuck her index finger in "1" and pulled the rotary dial until it ratcheted back. Punching out a quick ten digits would have been easier. The old-fashioned phone gave her too much time to think, worrying the same sore spot that hurt every time she called Richie.

She loved her little brother. She knew she'd done all she could for him. It was no reflection on her if his friends knew more; they'd been working this crisis for years. What hurt was that after ten years out there, they were more Richie's family than she was.

He picked up on the fifth ring. "Hello?"

"You're home."

"Where would I be, the opera?"

"Are you okay?"

He laughed that familiar chuckle. She shut her eyes tight. What would she do when he was gone?

"I'm watching the play-offs. What's up? Bored to tears in your woodsy retreat?"

"Hardly." She sighed. "You know the routine."

"Okay, okay. My T cells are holding their own, the chemo was hell, Bill got me a joint to deal with the nausea—of course, you didn't hear that from me—and I'm the same dashingly handsome rogue you've known since I was in diapers."

"You weren't so dashing in diapers, pipsqueak."

"I can hear the sibling rivalry now. You never adapted to being a displaced only child."

"Call it the eldest child's sense of responsibility. I gotta look after you, kid."

"You did a good job, Bridey. I just didn't want you hanging around here. I'm not the most patient patient."

She peered at the ceiling, picturing her latest. "Could be worse."

"Now, guilt assuaged, medical status reported, tell me why you called."

"I need some advice."

"The doctor's in."

"That's exactly what I need. What do you know about gun wounds." She listened to the pause. The raucous cheers of a sporting event faded in the background, the wonders of remote control.

"Playing with firearms, sis?"

"Playing with people who do. A man was hurt, he came to the door."

"And you let him in?" He sounded as outraged as Ben had when she'd put down her useless gun.

"This isn't the big city. I'm fine." She filled him in

on the rest of the details, omitting the farce with the dusty derringer.

"And I thought the Upper Peninsula was boring," Richie concluded wryly. "So run it by me again. What's the reason for not calling an ambulance?"

She shrugged, wincing when she realized how weak her answer would sound. The telephone cord trailed behind her as she carried the phone from one end of the kitchen to the other. "Because he asked me not to."

"That's a reason?"

"Hey, it was you who taught me to respect people's wishes, especially when—"

He caught her pause. "Especially when they're dying. Is he that bad?"

"No, but . . . He was scared. There was something about him."

"Always a good reason to let weirdos in your house."

"Richie."

"Is he dangerous?"

"Uh—"

"Bridey?"

"Only when he has to be." She didn't know where that insight came from, but the moment she said it she knew she'd happened on a truth.

To Richie's credit, he didn't laugh. Her brother's respect for her instincts never ceased to move her. Her last ex-boyfriend would've sneered her off the planet. That's why he was an ex, she supposed. "There's something about him, as if he'd steeled himself to things. He's determined. He won't tell me what really happened. But he's not dangerous, not to me."

"Did he swear to it?"

There it was, the faint disdain she'd braced herself for. "I need information, Richie, not attitude."

"Do I look like a medical reference?"

"You've got more doctors in your black book than Madonna has boyfriends."

"Let me see who I can reach. I'll have one of them call."

"Thanks."

"This isn't like love at first sight, is it?" Trust her brother to pick up vibes.

She hoped against hope Ben wasn't as perceptive. She searched for a logical definition of an intuitive hunch. "It's more like trust at first sight. Can you understand that?"

He mulled it over. "I think so."

She sighed. "Thanks, little brother."

"So what's he look like?"

She grinned. "Gorgeous."

"Mm-hmm."

"Black hair, fit as a Stradivarius, sexy as strawberries in champagne."

"And you've got him locked in a bedroom? Way to go, girl. You said he likes pain?"

"Funny. He's fighting it with everything he's got."

"Which sounds substantial."

"I wouldn't know," she replied tartly. "I just wish there was more I could do to help."

"That's you to a tee. By the way, my massage therapist swears there are pressure points in the feet that relieve pain."

"I'll bear that in mind." She pursed her lips at the thought of Richie in pain. "You going to be okay?"

"I'm going to be wonderful! How about you?"

"Living life with a capital *L* just like you told me to. Have that doctor call me."

"I will. And let me know *your* medical news."

"When there is some." She hung up. For an entire evening she'd forgotten one of her main reasons for being there. She smoothed her jersey over her flat stomach. Waiting was always the hardest part.

A telephone rang somewhere in the distance. Ben bolted awake. Pain clutched his ribs like barbed wire. He dragged in a breath, ground out a curse, and leaned back on his elbow. He was naked. His leg throbbed. He tried sitting up more slowly. The ringing stopped.

He ran a hand over his face. From the stubble's sandpapery rasp he reckoned it was past midnight. He strafed the room with a glare. The bed was a double, the lamp a tacky artifact, its gold shade covered with cutouts of bounding deer. Birch logs lined the walls, rustic and white. Bridget was gone.

He cursed. Lifting his leg off the bed, pain rolled through him. He waited for his head to clear. He was trapped. And all because he'd believed in her long enough to let down his guard and fall asleep.

Real caring had mingled with cool efficiency when she'd dabbed at his scratches. No way she was in league with the drug runners. He could have *sworn* she wouldn't betray him.

But misguided honesty could be equally deadly. She might play good citizen and call the police. Who knew how many members of the local force had been corrupted by easy money? Life was hard this far north. Until he knew who was in on the cargo shipments he couldn't trust anyone—not local lawmen, not hospital personnel.

Nevertheless, he should have told her how critical it was that no one find him. Then again, why should she trust him? She was a smart, wary, savvy woman with a sympathetic streak he'd played like a fiddle. He'd lied to her more than once since he'd gotten there, and she knew it. His conscience pained him along with his wound when he pictured how she must see him.

"You've been lying like a bad toupee, brother." Undercover he'd looked a dozen men in the eye and lied about everything from his name to his motives to his fictional criminal past. Around women he usually stuck to the values of honesty, honor, and integrity. Not that those qualities always rated with the fair sex. They certainly hadn't with Carla.

He threw back the covers and examined the bandage on his thigh. Nothing seeped through. Maybe it made sense that memories of his ex-wife haunted him. "Your life isn't flashing before your eyes, just your mistakes."

He'd been a lousy husband, providing for his family financially, never there emotionally. Or so Carla always claimed. He'd let her take Molly. His daughter would be six this year. It'd be four years since he'd seen her. There was a picture of her in his wallet. Where was it?

He didn't have the strength to search. Pain coursed through him with every heartbeat. He tried getting comfortable, picking out memories for distraction, discarding them just as fast.

He didn't indulge regrets. He'd made his choices. Finding out he wasn't cut out for family life had been a tough lesson to learn, but he'd learned it. Permanently. He'd also learned to work undercover, live by his wits, go with whatever the situation warranted. Trusting people wasn't his long suit. Making them trust him was vital.

A key rattled in the lock. He heard her mutter. A soft shoe kicked at the door. Something thumped. After a moment of silence the door burst open and Bridget stumbled halfway into the room. "Oh. You're awake." She dangled a ring of keys. "These skeleton things are useless."

"Thanks for the warning." To earn someone's trust, one had to show trust. He made the first move. "Thanks. For everything. I mean it."

"Anytime. Not that you should make a habit of this." She held an armful of afghan. Stepping into the hall, she dragged a rocker inside, placing it to the right of the bed. She got cozy, apparently settling in for the long haul.

"Weren't you sitting over there before?"

"We moved you to this side, don't you remember? You didn't want to sleep on the wet spot."

"Who does?"

"Your clothes were soaked—"

"I knew what you meant. Not that I'd be up for anything else. So to speak."

She smiled, her expression straightforward and sincere. Too candid? Too innocent? Her head canted slightly. She might be listening for something—sirens, a knock on the door.

He stared hard.

"Is there anything I can do? Open a window?"

"No." She could keep him alive—but only if he could trust her. "So where are we?"

"Paper Birch Lodge."

He scanned the white logs lining the walls. "Every room like this?"

"Some. It makes it a lot lighter than the usual log home. There are a few traditional rooms made out of local pine. Some plaster interior walls. You saw the outside, of course."

"Not really."

"You mean it didn't draw you like a beacon?"

He shook his head.

"It glows."

"It what?"

"In the moonlight. Or when it's lightning. From the lake it looks like a giant cruise ship thrown onto the bluff. It's the white birch."

"I didn't think you could build a house of birch."

"True, too soft. But you can paint the logs to resemble it, then panel the inside with the real thing. It's marvelous. Years ahead of its time. I'm looking at a historical designation."

"Big?"

"You really didn't see it."

All he'd seen was that lighted window. And her.

She gave him the rundown. "Twenty-six thousand square feet. Two floors with an attic above and a wine cellar below. Twenty bedrooms. A restaurant-size kitchen. Situated on eight hundred wilderness acres with one thousand feet of frontage on Bête Grise Bay."

"Been in your family long?"

"I wish. An auto magnate came up from Detroit around 1910 and fell in love with Copper Harbor. The Dodge Lodge, as it was originally called, was supposed to be a wedding present." A whimsical thought lit up her eyes. "Maybe that's why it's white."

She had a dimple in her right cheek and a bedrock sincerity. He was beginning to believe her lecture wasn't intended to drown out the sound of people approaching. "Go on."

"You should sleep."

"I can't."

She gnawed her lip in a gesture he recognized from before. "There's not much I can do for the pain."

"It's not so bad. Tell me more about the lodge." Maybe she'd let something slip.

"It's pretty remote. Rumor has it they shipped in whiskey from Canada during Prohibition."

Something like that, he thought.

"I haven't found any in the wine cellars." She laughed. "They're huge. Al Capone could have hid in them."

"Stuff like that goes on all the time. Smuggling, evading customs."

"Not much call for bathtub gin nowadays."

He studied her indulgent smile. No hesitation. No tension near the mouth. The woman couldn't have learned to lie convincingly in the last couple hours. He tried another one. "Why don't you open the window?"

"You're sure? Okay. We'll see how chilly it is."

She hadn't jumped at the chance. Neither had she argued against it. Something eased in his chest.

Sitting back down, she rocked comfortably.

"What happened after that?"

"To the lodge? The Dodge brothers died in the influenza epidemic of 1921. Mrs. Dodge was more interested in building Meadowbrook Hall. This place sat empty for most of the thirties and forties. There was a spurt of activity in the seventies, three owners in a row with grandiose plans. The locals began calling it Tax Dodge Lodge."

"And you?"

She fanned out her fingers as if reading off a marquee. "Paper Birch Lodge. That's what the brochure will say. Or White Birch Lodge. I haven't decided."

"Then you're not from around here?"

"My home base is Chicago. My company designs executive retreats, spas, conference centers. Have you ever been to an executive retreat?"

He could think of a few federal prisons that nearly qualified. "Let me guess. Tennis courts on every corner, financiers and stockbrokers hoeing the gardens."

Pleased with his teasing, she laughed and rocked forward. Elbows on her knees, she linked her fingers loosely. "Minus the golf course, that's what we want. Low-tech. Free-form. Canoes on the Montreal River, nature trails, biking, hiking. Mostly it will be a place for reflection and unwinding before the fireplace. Structured boredom, I call it."

"CEOs go in for that?"

"The trick is anticipating what the stressed-out executive needs instead of what they think they want."

"Which is?"

"To fill their daily planners with more activities. I saw this place and knew it was the perfect getaway."

His gaze shot to hers.

Lost in her vision, she barely noticed. "It's my own sneaky way of making people smell the roses. Roses they'd otherwise be cultivating, pricing, and discussing how to corner a market share of."

If she was crooked, he'd eat his socks. The more she talked the more he trusted her. And the more tired he got. At times he barely heard her murmuring voice over the lake's rumble.

"My first job is to redesign the rooms without losing the sense of rich-people-roughing-it. That was very popular in the Teddy Roosevelt era. I've been decorating, drawing up plans, even making some rough maps of the property. There are some old logging camps north of here. . . ." Her voice trailed off.

He snapped awake. He'd missed something.

"Are you okay?"

"Yeah, fine. You, uh, have colleagues?"

"Normally. This project's strictly my baby." She chuckled at a private joke and sat back, tucking her hands inside the afghan. "It's my own retreat. I estimate I'll be here six months at least."

Exhaustion crept up his limbs like vines around a ruin. He'd have suspected her of drugging him if a soft voice and perfume could be considered drugs. She'd just confided in him, the first step in establishing trust. "You're alone," he repeated.

"Don't get any ideas."

The ones he got didn't stay long. "Staying long?"

"Six months." Another bemused smile. She'd told him that.

"I meant, have you been here long?"

"Got here three weeks ago."

Couldn't be part of the gang. That was all he needed to know. "Sorry if I scared you."

"Gunshot wounds have to be reported to the police. Is that why you didn't want to go to the hospital?"

"I don't trust hospitals."

"A gun-toting Christian Scientist, eh?"

"Sarcasm. That I remember about you."

She chuckled. "Didn't know you were stuck with Nurse Ratchet, did you?"

She came at him, her face soft in the light, her eyes wide and brown, her smile beguiling. He told himself to be on guard. You never knew.

She tucked the sheet around his chest. "I think I'll sit here awhile. You go to sleep."

The thought comforted him and disturbed him in ways he couldn't define. "Did you call anyone?"

The light clicked off. Before it did he thought he caught a flicker of something in her expression. "I heard the phone ring," he said, his voice hard as slate in the dark.

"I called my brother," she answered. "Taking care of you made me think of him."

Her dying brother. He winced and hated himself for the cynicism that came with his job. All night long she'd been better to him than he deserved. "Sorry. Sorry for the trouble."

"Sleep tight."

Near dawn the pain doubled. He doubted he'd slept more than ten minutes at a stretch. He kept waking to the sight of her. She sat curled in her rocker. The afghan had slipped. The moon crept over the side of the house, caressing her milky shoulder in its white hand. Her faint breathing mingled with the sound of the waves on the shore.

He said her name, a whisper. She didn't stir. He said it again, this time like a prayer. She hadn't betrayed him. He knew that now. "Thank you."

FOUR

The juice spilled. The eggs burned. The toast took three tries.

She told herself it was cigarette nerves. "Three days and counting." She walked to the back door, threw it open, and drew in a lungful of pine-scented air.

One cigarette. One.

She slammed the door. The glass rattled. Striding to the counter, she popped a strawberry in her mouth. Healthy. Low-cal. Far superior to the smell of smoke—

"Smoke!" She yanked the pan off the stove, not before the oatmeal had burned to the bottom, forming a mysterious metal-bonded alloy it'd take a chisel to get out. She dumped what she could and let the rest soak in the soapstone sink. What she really wanted was to get that old-fashioned pump going. Some vigorous activity would take her mind off her cooking disaster—and off Ben.

He'd been awake most of the night. If it weren't

for the leg and the ribs, she suspected he'd have spent the hours tossing and turning. Instead, he'd speared her with long looks, concentrating all his attention on her. Every time a wisp of moonlight escaped through the clouds she saw his eyes lasering in, black beams warring with the moon's gauzy blue white.

He needed her. The resulting sensation disturbed her. However, she couldn't bail out simply because he made her uncomfortable. His look made her feel other things. Feathery rays of heat coursed beneath her skin, a silky awareness of every inch of her body. If the rocking chair had allowed it, she would've tossed and turned too.

"Bridget Bernard," she muttered in a warning tone. Restlessness dogged her like a yapping terrier. She blamed lack of sleep, too much excitement, too many nerves.

She dropped a piece of toast on the plate and licked butter from her fingertip. All she had to do was get a healthy man-size breakfast together. Before he finished it, she intended to find out more about him. It was one thing to house a hurt, helpless stranger. It was another letting a healthy, potentially dangerous man sleep under the same roof.

She breezed in, kicking a chair closer, humming a tune under her breath. Ben rubbed his shaggy, scratchy chin. His body felt achy and stiff in the few places where it didn't clutch in pain. He eased himself into a sitting position. She set the tray down, busily stuffing pillows behind him.

The bruised rib jolted pain through him. He took

a deep breath to get through it. Her scent filled his lungs.

A recent shower had left a dewiness on her skin. The scent of shampoo and soap curled through him, eliciting thoughts he instantly squelched. Her breast skimmed his shoulder as she fluffed a final pillow.

"There," she said.

He sat back.

She wore a roomy peach-colored sweater over a low-necked white T-shirt. White stretch pants outlined her calves. She proudly picked up the tray from the end of the bed. "Hope you're not a vegetarian."

"Do I look like one?" He captured her gaze and held it when it would have veered away.

She took up his dare. "You look groggy, mangy, ornery, and hungry. But no, you do *not* look like a vegetarian."

"Thanks."

She hefted the tray. "I thought a little red meat would be good for you."

"The bloodier the better."

"I didn't haul it out of the woods raw. It has seen a frying pan." She set it in place.

He tried not to bump it with his knees. "Are you always this perky in the morning?"

"Hardly. And I hate that word."

"I'll try not to use it."

Something wasn't right. A buzz energized her. She wouldn't look at him longer than a New York minute. Her gaze flitted over the food, the floor, the mirror above the dresser. When she caught his reflection studying her she looked away.

He would've blamed it on being naked under these covers, but a bandage wound round half his chest and she'd said herself he looked like roadkill. He flattered himself if he thought it had anything to do with sexual attraction. Maybe her nervousness had another cause. Like guilt.

She parted the curtains. Was that a signal? He silently cursed. He hated the way his profession taught him to evaluate everyone he came in contact with. He'd decided the previous night he could trust her. In the light of day they started from scratch.

He scanned the room. He needed to know the layout of this place so he could get to a telephone. He had to report in, warn his case officer their surveillance had been compromised and he'd been put out of commission for the time being.

Running out of excuses to keep her back to him, she perched on the rocker's edge, bouncing rhythmically. "You haven't touched your breakfast."

"I'm getting there."

"Feeling better?"

"Getting there."

"How's your leg?"

"Feels like an elephant gnawed on it."

"If you, uh, need help getting to the bathroom."

"I'll manage." Or die trying. He wanted the focus back on her. He picked up a fistful of cutlery. "Do I make you nervous?"

She shook her head. Her hair swished a denial. "Withdrawal."

His face felt like flint. "What?"

"Cigarettes." She held her hand out parallel with the tray. Her fingers trembled. Point made, she snitched one of the strawberries from the bowl she'd brought. "Three days. Seventy-two hours. Sixty cigarettes I haven't smoked."

"Pack a day, huh?"

"Used to be. 'Think of yourself as an *ex*-smoker.' That's rule number one." She stole strawberry number two.

It would account for most of her restlessness, he thought. Her gaze strafed the tray, the nubby bedspread, the iron bedframe. He raised his good knee. She looked out the window, hugging one knee to her chest as she rocked harder.

He looked at the mist-coated treetops hemming them in. "Is this the back of the house?"

"Mm-hm. The lake's on that side." She hitched a thumb toward the door.

Vertical lodge poles framed it in white. Birch logs lined the walls horizontally. Smaller diagonal lengths held up the peaked ceiling. "Twenty rooms?"

"Twenty bedrooms. Twenty-eight rooms overall, not counting servants' quarters over the garage."

"How many cars?"

"My Jeep and a 'twenty-eight Dodge that doesn't run."

"Big place."

"Granot Loma's bigger, near Marquette. But this is a beauty."

So was she. He caught himself staring. She flushed. He sorted out the silverware and prepared to dig in. The sight of two eggs over easy hit him like a sledgehammer to the solar plexus. He glared at the slab of steak, the golden oil slick on the toast. The curled bacon was done just the way he liked it, crunchy on the outside, chewy down the middle. If he put it in his mouth, he'd vomit.

"So how far are we from town?" He nudged the plate away, hoping the scent wouldn't reach him.

Her eyes grew wide. "Would you prefer oatmeal? Cereal? There's fresh fruit—" She'd put fresh melon in with the strawberries.

His saliva curdled at the thought of mushy food. "No thanks. It takes me a while to get started in the morning."

"That's leaded coffee."

"I'll get to it." He'd lost the chance to ask about town without making her suspicious. "What about you? You're a decorator?"

"I design executive retreats. You don't remember much from last night?"

"I had a few other things on my mind."

"Such as?"

She waited him out. She was good at it. He was forced to eat a grainy piece of toast to cover while he got his story straight. "Being a damn fool with a gun, for starters. Bleeding to death. Making a fool of myself in front of you." He looked her in the eye. That should be sufficient to chase her off.

She played with a loose string on her sweater.

"You're redesigning this?"

"As little as possible," she insisted. "There are certain amenities we can't do without. Better hot water. Television. We'll have to hide the satellite dish with landscaping. Personally I'd do without TV, but CNN is essential for the clientele. They'll want computer access, faxes, E-mail, modems. I hate the idea of someone on vacation sneaking off to *work*. However, we've found the best thing to do is let them know the technology's here, like a security blanket, then limit access except in emergencies."

"How do you do that?"

"Cut the phone lines."

He swallowed hard. "There's gotta be a telephone here somewhere."

She laughed. "I was joking. We have one downstairs, an ancient rotary. And there's my portable."

"And where's that?" he asked casually, cutting off a chunk of meat.

"Who knows? Next time it rings I'll find it."

Not if he found it first.

She tucked her foot under her and leaned forward, a concerned look on her face. "Speaking of which, I should warn you—"

He looked up slowly. What had she done now?

"Once I get started working I become oblivious to everything else. There've been days I've looked up and noticed it was dark already. If I forget you're here, feel free to yell." She chewed her lower lip. "Maybe I could bring you a bell or something."

"Working until dark sounds suspiciously like workaholic behavior."

"You mean I'm as bad as the executives I'm trying to slow down? It helps to know how they justify those endless hours. Besides, sometimes work *is* fun."

Not his. Nevertheless, the more he knew of her routine the better. He cut another thin slice of meat. It was going down, that's all he could say for it. "So you get absorbed in things."

"I flit. If one project isn't humming, I move on to the next."

Bridget watched him pick at his food. His body was as fine as she remembered, but his color wasn't good. She'd wanted to find out more about him. But that's when she'd been worried about a healthy stranger under her roof. She had nothing to fear from him for another day at least. The man could barely chew.

While he recuperated, talking about her work was a harmless diversion. After three weeks of even the most luxurious solitary confinement, it was nice finding someone to listen.

She counted her duties on her fingers. "As an architect I decide which walls to knock out. We're converting a few bedrooms to bathrooms and suites. As a decorator I still haven't decided which styles to draw from and how to mix-and-match them."

"You like the decorating best."

"How would you know?"

"Your eyes light up when you talk about it."

She didn't have time to ponder the sensation fluttering in her chest. She hadn't realized he'd been paying such close attention. "Actually, I wasn't trained in it. It's probably my biggest challenge. I'm terrible at visualizing. It's strictly hands-on. I lay out swatches, paste up wallpaper. Live with it awhile. When I get tired of painting and pasting there's always public relations. I'm writing the brochure too."

"A little of everything."

"Keeps life interesting." Not nearly as interesting as her gunshot guest. "So what do you do for fun, Mister—"

"Ben."

She crooked a brow.

He chewed his toast, drank some juice, and swallowed. "Renfield."

"What do you do for pleasure and/or profit, Mr. Renfield?"

"Are we that formal all of a sudden?"

"We don't have to be."

"Then Ben's fine." He drained the juice. He still hadn't answered her question. "Which rooms are you working in now?"

"These." She waved a hand toward the hall. "I don't have a set itinerary—too Type A. If I get bored at my drawing board, I move to a room. If my eyes cross from looking at too many swatches, I go to my laptop and work on the brochure."

"All the while *not* smoking."

She'd been gnawing a fingernail. "Thanks." She sneaked another strawberry. A small pile of green stems littered the tray's corner. "At this rate I'll weigh three hundred pounds."

He raked her body with typical male disdain. "You can't be obsessed with your weight."

"Believe me, I'm not. When you've seen enough people with AIDS, thin doesn't look so chic. I just figured, with the baby, I'd add enough weight as it is. I don't want to throw in another twenty pounds on top of that."

"Baby?"

"I'm pregnant. That's why I quit smoking."

That did it. Breakfast was over. "You're what? You never said—" There's no way he'd have put her *and* a baby in danger. He *had* to get to a phone. He slid the tray as far down the bed as his arm could reach.

"I'm hoping," she explained. "Nothing's certain yet."

He relaxed by a slim margin. His breath hitched in his lungs as he sat back. He should have seen it coming. A beautiful woman. She had to be married. Though if he were her husband, he'd never let her stay so isolated. Not that he knew anything about being a good husband. Or about her. "You're married, then."

"No."

"Engaged."

"Not really."

He settled for the wishy-washy modern term. "Involved, then."

Dark hair swished softly over her shoulders as she shook her head. "Actually, I've never met the man."

Had he missed something? "Then how?"

"Artificial insemination," she replied blithely.

"Look, I've got to get to a phone. Do you have one? That portable would be good. I have to make a call." He would've lurched out of bed if he hadn't been buck naked. This was what he got for lying his way through life—trapped in a remote lodge with a certified kook.

"If I'd known it would upset you, I wouldn't have mentioned it," she said, blissfully unconcerned with the scowl on his face. "I only had the procedure done three weeks ago. Before I came here."

"Procedure? Is that what they call it?"

"That's what it is. Funny, when you didn't give me a hard time about my brother I assumed you were something of a liberal."

"Assume again."

She grinned, her cheeks blushing becomingly. He would have called it demure if they hadn't been discussing what they were discussing.

"You're a conservative, then?" she asked.

"Newt Gingrich is president of the ACLU compared to me."

"Which I'm sure makes you the best judge of what I should do with my life." She dawdled over his tray, munching his uneaten bacon, dabbing her lips with a spare napkin, waiting for him to put another foot in his mouth.

"I don't want to aruge," he rasped out. "I just want a phone."

"As they say in the song, 'Who you gonna call?' "

"That's my business."

"It's my phone."

"Look—" As if his broken ribs weren't enough, pain speared through his thigh when he shifted. "Bring me some of those clothes you talked about, and I'll be on my way."

"It isn't that awful."

"You've got enough problems without me."

"Mental problems?" she asked wryly.

"Your life is your business."

"Thank you."

He stifled a groan as she sat at the foot of the bed. She wasn't going anywhere until she explained.

"When my brother told me to go out and live life, I started thinking about what I really wanted. A baby was right up there, top of the list. I'd put it off partly because I was consumed with my career, but mostly because I was waiting."

"For what?"

"The husband, the lover, the usual things that precede having a baby. Like marriage."

"I'm familiar with it."

"So I thought, why wait? Why let my chance of having a baby go by while I wait for life to provide me with the perfect mate? I decided to get impregnated on my own. Sperm banks. Doctors. It's not exactly romantic, but it's the goal not the process that counts."

"I'd say the process is half the fun."

She grinned. "It's good to have a sense of humor about it."

If she thought he found this funny, the woman wasn't paying attention.

"I should know in a week or so whether it 'took' or not."

"The implantation."

"Insemination. Implantation is when they fertilize the egg in a dish, then implant it. Insemination is—"

"Do you mind? I just ate."

Her laugh would've startled him—if anything she could have said or done at that moment could have startled him further.

She gave him a sweetly sympathetic look and lowered her voice. "I haven't shocked you, have I?"

Shock? Hell, he'd worked undercover for years. He'd seen plenty. But the idea of this desirable, bright, animated woman getting pregnant by a, a what, a needle—?

"You are shocked."

"Try appalled. Mortified. Disgusted. You name it. Any man with two eyes would want to get you pregnant."

"He'd need something besides two eyes."

"A working third leg, then." He shook his head, slaking back an unruly lock of greasy hair. He needed shampoo. He needed a shave and a shower and a phone call. Even prisoners were allowed one call. "What are you smiling at?" he growled.

"More to the point, what are we arguing about?"

"It's your life, sweetheart."

"Yes, it is."

"I'm just telling you, there's adoption. There are babies out there."

"They wouldn't be mine."

"And some stranger's is?"

"Half-mine."

"Half-yours, half–test tube."

"I want to carry on the family line."

"You and Mr. Gene Pool."

"I'd rather have a baby *without* a husband than marry a man I don't love just to have a baby."

"Then look for a better man—" The louder his voice got, the softer hers became.

"I have."

"How?" His arm motioned to the room, the lodge, the world. "How do you expect to find a man in the middle of the nowhere damn Upper Peninsula?"

"You're getting worked up, Ben."

"I'm just telling you—"

"And telling me and telling me. I won't tell you how to live your life, you don't tell me how to live mine. Besides"—she lightly tapped his bad leg—"my life seems to be going a lot smoother than yours lately."

"Until the rabbit dies," he muttered.

She headed for the door.

He sat forward to give her more what for. The pain gripped him like an eagle's talon. He gritted his teeth until it passed.

She turned in the doorway, fishing a key from her pocket.

"That old skeleton lock isn't going to hold me," he warned.

"Neither is your left leg. I'll check in on you around lunchtime, okay? And Ben, it isn't contagious. There's nothing to worry about, honest."

He muttered his opinion on that score as the door clicked shut. He didn't give a hoot what she did with her life. She was obviously some wacko who only passed for sensible and alluring.

What burned him was the idea he might have put her in danger. The smugglers could come looking today. Rain would've washed away any blood trail; they couldn't *know* his whereabouts. Then again, checking the only house in the area wasn't out of the question. If they came to the door, she wouldn't know enough to lie.

Not unless she'd picked up that talent from him.

Right. And Bridget wanting a manufactured baby made sense.

"In a parallel universe."

She opened the door and stepped lightly to the foot of the bed before he could wipe the scowl off his face. "If you get bored, I thought you'd like something to read."

She'd given him way too much to think about already, none of it central to his predicament.

"Stephen King. One of my favorites." She gave him a wink, then traipsed to the door. "It's about this woman who finds an injured man and takes him in. He's a writer, so she forces him to write a book with an ending *she* likes."

He caught on quick. "And if this baby thing doesn't take, you're going to put *me* into stud service?"

Her wicked chuckle echoed down the hall. "Now, there's an idea."

He fingered the book's spine. *Misery*. Nothing could have been more appropriate.

FIVE

Bridget unrolled the wallpaper. Masking tape held it in place while she stepped back and considered it. When the logs in the other rooms became too heavy for guests to look at, flowery prints on the few plaster walls might be soothing. Or would male clients prefer patterns and geometrics? She ought to ask Ben.

"So much for forgetting he's here." Working through the morning, she'd succeeded for minutes on end in not thinking of him. Except when she turned on her tape deck and wondered if he liked classical music. Or when she opened the window and wondered if he'd prefer a bedroom on this side of the house, with the lake shimmering like diamonds. He seemed like a doer not a muser.

She caught herself staring at the view, humming Sinatra, Sade, something slow-moving and sultry. She found herself smiling for the tenth time in an hour.

He'd gone downright ballistic when she mentioned the pregnancy. "Hypothetical pregnancy," she reminded herself. Nothing would be certain for a week at least. Even then, things could go wrong.

Ben would be long gone by that time. She found that hard to imagine. He'd made such an impression on her life in so short a time. A breath of a breeze blew in from the woods. She recalled the damp forest scent of his clothes the night before, the musky aroma of his skin that morning. She unrolled wallpaper and thought of his bandages, a tight band of white around his chest. She no longer worried about ambulances. However, considering his pale look over breakfast, she felt safe leaving him alone for a few hours.

"Define 'safe.' "

Plopping down cross-legged on the floor, she flipped through a decorating book and found herself idly brushing her chin with a bristly strand of hair. Her clothes felt loose and flimsy. The day had warmed up fast. She'd ditched the sweater for a silky tunic. Shorts draped between her thighs. She stared at a Gothic Revival drawing room knowing full well it had nothing to do with her project. Something was nagging at her.

Not something she realized, nothing. It was what Ben *hadn't* said that bothered her. Never once had he suggested getting in touch with his family. All he had to have said was that someone somewhere needed to hear from him, and she would've sprinted for that telephone. He hadn't mentioned a living soul, not a wife, or a girlfriend.

Who worried about him? Who would rush to take care of him? She understood about Richie's friends; some had family who refused even to speak to them. Ben hadn't asked for anyone. He seemed completely alone and content to stay that way.

She flipped the page. Rattan was too kitschy and Mission style too heavy. Her worrying about Ben Renfield was as out of place as his outrage over her method of getting pregnant. The circumstances of their meeting had loosed her imagination until it ran wild.

She smoothed the fabric of her shirt over her stomach, patting it absently. She had work to do and another life to care about besides Ben's.

He collapsed against the doorjamb. So much for escape attempts. He'd made it to the bathroom, determined to clear his head with a splash of cold water. After that he'd half hopped, half dragged himself to the door. She hadn't locked it. That saved him one problem.

Staggering the length of the hall in search of the telephone proved tougher with every door he passed. Twenty bedrooms. He lurched past six.

The walls spun. The papery birch whispered as he put out a hand for support. He'd always thought this stuff was white. Up close, splashes of yellows and pink ran through it.

That must be the reason she'd looked so good against it, he thought. The yellows gave a golden glow to her midnight hair and brown eyes, the pinks lent warmth to her softly tinted cheeks. He remembered her sitting on the bed, laughing at him as he sputtered like Archie Bunker over her baby arrangement. What the hell did he care, he hardly knew the woman.

It irked him every time he pictured it. He felt his mouth harden and his fists clench.

He pushed on another step. His leg was on fire,

the muscles threatening to seize up. Served him right for fantasizing about someone he should never have met, a woman he shouldn't have gotten involved in this mess.

Breezes from the lake swished curtains to his right. A tangy pine scent permeated the rooms to his left. The bandage around his chest grew damp with sweat. The knotted towel around his hips sagged as he drew in a breath. The hall stretched longer than a football field. He still hadn't found her damn phone.

He peered in the next room and found her. She stood in front of a row of plain windows, their dated curtains in a pile at her feet. Dust motes swirled in the air. She climbed a step stool, slinging fabric over the curtain rod, fluffling the folds, stepping down to assess.

She hummed along with a radio, a half smile playing over her lips. Flattening a long blouse over her hips, her thumbs splayed on her lower back, fingers pointed at the ground. They tapped her rear end in time to the music.

A hot sensation, vague but insistent, pulsed in Ben's lower body. Another sensation, infinitely sweeter, curiously painful, built in his chest. There was something utterly feminine and slightly off-kilter about everything she did, from homemaking for strangers to nest feathering for a manufactured pregnancy.

She stared at the open books littering the floor, nudging one with her toe. She'd been good to him, automatically, generously, even foolishly. He wanted to pay her back.

When she hopped back up the ladder, he staggered out of sight of the door. His job didn't allow for intimacy. To hear Carla tell it, that extended to his private life, his whole personality. A year before the divorce she'd found someone to fill the weeks he was away. He'd taken the responsibility for their failed marriage the way he took on any other tough job. He shouldered it alone, never mind if it took two to wreck a marriage.

The telephone rang.

He cursed silently but vehemently. Blundering toward the bedroom across the hall, he ducked inside. Paint cans lay piled and scattered. Wallpaper rolls and fabric books sat stacked on old newspapers and plastic drop cloths. He listened to her stomp down the hall toward the source of the ringing.

"I know you're here somewhere," she muttered.

The crash punctuated the third ring. Bridget whirled. She'd been zeroing in on her portable when a clatter of tin and a grunt of pain stopped her in her tracks. She raced the other way.

Her first thought was that a raccoon had gotten in; not likely on the second floor. Craning her neck around the doorframe, she found Ben sprawled beside a slip-covered chair. She crouched by his side. "Are you all right?"

He muttered something obscene into the plastic.

"What happened?"

Facedown, he spread his hands on the floor. His back muscles bunched.

"Don't tell me," she said wryly. "The marine in you wanted to do push-ups."

The veins on his arms stood out. He lifted himself far enough to fold his good leg under him, turn over onto his hip, and sit up. Draping his arm over his raised knee, he bowed his head, panting for breath.

Bridget fought every instinct not to hover. Fresh blood soaked through the bandage on his thigh. A towel bunched in his lap. Lank black hair fell around his cheekbones. She caught sight of her hand halfway there and drew it back. "Better?"

He took a breath to answer and winced. "Your phone stopped ringing."

"What were you doing out of bed?"

"You forgot to take me on the tour."

She tried her best schoolmarm tone. "You barely ate this morning; you lost I don't know how much blood last night—"

"I didn't eat all my vegetables. I know; it's my fault I fell down." The fury on his face would have chased off lesser mortals.

Bridget recognized it for what it was. No man liked being helpless, especially in front of a woman. She planted her hands on her thighs, elbows at right angles. "I can help you back to bed, or you can sit here and feel sorry for yourself."

He met her gaze. "I'll sit."

"You are the orneriest, least cooperative patient I've ever dealt with. If you don't stay in bed, I'm going to strap you down."

"Could be fun."

"Don't cross me, Benjamin." She sat Indian-style, the floorboards cool beneath her thighs. "Tell me when you're ready to get moving, and we'll go."

"I need to make a call."

"Family?"

"I don't have family."

That's what she'd been afraid of. She remained stern, idly examining a thumbnail. "Wife?"

"Divorced."

"Mother?"

"Dead."

"Father?"

"Gone since I was ten. Can you skip the questions about my family tree and just bring me the damn phone?"

She relaxed. Her shoulders lowered and her mouth widened in a shadow of a smile. Damn her, Ben thought. How was it every time he raised his voice the woman seemed downright relieved? He didn't intimidate her at all.

He brusquely gripped the chair arm and hauled himself to a standing position. The towel tumbled.

Her hand shot out, trapping it against his groin. Just as quickly, she jerked her hand away.

If he'd had a free hand, he would've grabbed it as it fell. If his left leg worked better he could have pinned it between his thighs. No such luck.

Bridget swept the towel off the floor. Scrambling to her feet, she made a show of flipping her hair off her face, as if it had blocked her view all this time. She looked him in the eye—nowhere else. "Here."

He let it hang there—the towel, that is. "I need both hands to hold on to this chair. My balance isn't good."

Her ability to look him unwaveringly in the eye wasn't so hot either.

Apparently the woman hated dares. She stepped breast to chest, swung one end of the towel around his backside, caught it the first time, and handed the rest over to him.

"Aren't you going to tuck it in?" he asked.

"I think you can manage that."

"If I try, it might drop."

Oh, she didn't like that. He suppressed a grin. She tucked the very tip beside his navel. He sucked in his abdomen. Vanity, thy name is man.

"There. Your modesty is preserved." She picked up toppled paint cans. "Not that you have anything to be modest about," she muttered.

"You noticed."

She redoubled her neatening. "I've been playing at this nursing stuff for months. Men are men."

"And some are better than others." He felt weak, clumsy, incompetent. He needed a shave and a bath. He certainly didn't feel like a man a woman would blush over. If he told her the real reason he was there, she'd probably laugh him off the face of the planet. Mr. Superhero Secret Agent. If he hadn't stepped on that twig, he'd never have drawn their attention, never gotten shot—

Never seen her blush. Her lashes fluttered on her cheeks. She wet her lips with a sweep of her tongue. She waited, flustered about how to proceed. She couldn't very well force him to bed. He reached out an arm.

She went to him, ready to help any way she could. He didn't deserve it, but that didn't stop him from taking advantage of her kindness. Gripping the chair with one hand, he buried the other in her hair. Weighing soft waves in his palm, his fingers burrowed to the warmth of her scalp.

Her eyes widened, still locked with his. He'd felt the back of her hand tremble against his abdomen when she'd fumbled that knot in place. He wanted to feel the rest of her tremble. Just once.

"Are you okay?"

"I've been better." His thigh throbbed, the bruise thudded, and the towel barely hid his baser desires. "You still have to get me to bed."

"You'll have to lean on me." She stepped under his arm to support him.

"I was kind of looking forward to it."

Bridget hoisted his arm over her shoulder once more. "We can do it. Don't fold on me yet." She'd left him at the foot of the bed, his hand curving over the iron frame as she yanked down the covers. Bloodstains from the night before had turned rusty brown. Wrinkles look cast in concrete. She wasn't dealing with the princess and the pea here. Nevertheless— "Can you wait while I change the sheets?"

He nodded, hair sticking to his forehead in wet slashes.

She rushed from bedroom to linen closet and back. She barely got the fitted sheet on when he swayed. "I'll tuck the rest in around you. Come on."

He opened his eyes and concentrated. He'd dropped the pretend seductiveness after the first three steps. She helped him navigate the bedside.

"I can make it." He'd been saying that all the way down the hall.

She tried to believe it. "Just one more." To get him onto the bed without pinning his left leg beneath him, she'd have to turn him around.

"Bridget?"

"Why can't I figure this out? If you stand here, and I move here—"

"Bridget."

She looked up. His head bent toward her. His lips paused inches from hers.

Events unfolded in slow motion. Thoughts, emotions, and sensations tumbled through her mind double speed. She splayed both hands on his chest. His skin was clammy, cool on the surface, feverish underneath. The muscles bunched beneath her palm. A subterranean heat tantalized it. She tried standing him up straighter.

He kept coming. She felt his breath on her face, saw his eyes flutter shut. Exhilaration shot through her. Anticipation. She took a quick breath, ashamed, excited. He was going to kiss her. Her knees felt as watery as the blood in her veins. It was crazy. And too deliciously unsettling to deny. Life was short and emotions weren't safer if thought out beforehand.

Looking up at him, she whispered his name. Her lips slightly parted.

His unshaven face brushed hers with a rasp. His arms came around her, his body pressing into her. One leg parted hers, nudging her thighs apart.

Her mind lagged behind her melting body, telling her nipples not to bud, her breath not to shudder in and out of her lungs. She didn't know what to do.

Ben did. He leaned forward, bending her back until the backs of her thighs touched the mattress. She let out a startled cry and they both sprawled onto the bed. His body pinned hers.

"Sorry," he said with a groan.

"All this time I thought you were making a pass, not passing out!"

"Don't move."

"I don't think I can."

His chest heaved. Her breasts ached. She pretended it was from the weight.

"Am I too heavy?" he asked.

He'd move if she said so. Weak as he was, she'd move heaven and earth not to hurt him. "I'll be fine. Can you just lift up a little?"

He planted his elbows outside her shoulders and raised up slightly. She wriggled upward until her chin cleared his shoulder. "That's better."

They lay there for minutes while he rested. She tried to chase off the unwarranted image of a man spent from making love, his body collapsed on hers, their hearts beating in rhythm. A drop of sweat trickled down his ribs. She wiped it off with her thumb, dabbing it on the bandage, vaguely realizing she'd wrapped her arms around him. She set her hands primly on either side of his ribs. "Are you okay?" she whispered.

"I will be. I just need to rest."

"That's okay." She stared at the ceiling. It was fine. Really. She should have given him more time to rest before bringing him back to his room. Next time she found him on the floor somewhere, she'd drag the whole bed—frame, box springs, mattress, and pillows—to wherever he was.

Gradually his breathing eased. His chin brushed her collarbone. His breath feathered alongside her neck. Tension seeped into her limbs, a nagging ache that made her want to move.

She stayed still. "So, how about them Tigers?"

He laughed a gritty laugh. "Another minute, okay? Then I'll get out of your hair."

It wasn't her hair she was worried about. Except when he played his fingertips through it.

She turned her head to the side. He stopped.

"I don't usually fall on women I don't know."

She had to get both their minds off where they were. Placing her arms around him in a friendly hug, she grinned up at him. "You barely ate, you lost a lot of blood, what did you expect after three hours' sleep?"

"We're trained—" He stopped.

Bridget counted the logs surrounding the light fixture overhead. "Trained for what?"

He played with the red highlights in her hair. Tingles slithered through her, starting at her scalp and whispering their way down her neck.

"I meant my mother should have trained me better," he said.

"Ah." Another lie, she thought distantly. She ought to be angry, to feel threatened.

She felt his ribs beneath the bandage. The hair on his legs crinkled against her thigh. She felt the towel bunched between them; her squirming had dragged it upward. At its hem nothing came between them except her flimsy summer shorts. There was nothing flimsy about him.

She closed her eyes, chasing off the flash of skin she'd seen when she'd picked up his towel. Images were nothing compared with physical impressions. He was thick and hot, his skin satiny. A dull throb built against her inner thigh, met inside by a pool of heat.

His thumb brushed her cheekbone. She opened her eyes. She didn't remember having closed them. She didn't remember his eyes being so blue, so turbulent. They matched the color of the lake on a cold sunny day, storm clouds gathering.

He nuzzled her cheek with his nose, his words soft as sin. "I'm not hurting you, am I?"

"I'm fine."

"I wouldn't hurt you, Bridget. I want you to know that. You're not in danger."

She was. Her heart cracked for something she'd told herself she didn't need. "Roll over."

"I kind of like where I am."

That purely male grin should have relieved her. Black hair made him look devilishly sexy. Sheer exhaustion made him look wickedly indolent. They could have been lovers sharing a bed in the afternoon, disheveled and drained.

"I hate thinking about it," he said.

She thought a mile a minute, most of it X-rated. "Hate what?"

"The idea of you pregnant and alone. Not even a father to sue for support—"

"Would you *quit* that!" Bridget shoved him away. He yelped in pain.

She yelped in alarm. "I'm sorry. I didn't mean that."

"Then don't move."

"I'm sorry. Your ribs—"

"I believe you."

She held her breath while he caught his. His nearness assaulted her on every side. She couldn't take a breath without drawing his scent into her lungs. His lips hovered; she'd never tasted him. His touch caressed her from head to toe, more erotic for sheer stillness. Her bones themselves responded. She listened for his ragged breath and heard an intimate whisper.

"I'm sorry I yelled." He meant about the baby.

"You don't let go of things, do you?"

"I just couldn't understand a woman like you—"

A woman like her was in more trouble than she could say. He'd unconsciously adjusted his lower body, fitting it to the vee between her thighs.

"You should find someone," he said, "someone you can trust. There've got to be men—" A sigh scraped his throat.

Men? She imagined him in her, surrendering physically to his hoarse commands. She felt the seep of hot sticky honey between her thighs and nearly moaned. "What about this man?" she asked. "You still haven't told me who you are. What were you doing in the woods?"

Elbows supporting him, he lifted his head and looked down into her eyes. She would have held that look if he hadn't continued stroking her hair with both hands. Her eyes drifted shut. She forced them open. "Ben."

"What?" he whispered.

"You're not answering the question."

His gaze traced the side of her neck.

"Ben."

His lips parted. She felt his tongue ripple over her lower lip, prod sweetly at the corner of her mouth. "What do you want to know?"

Oh, little things, she thought. Like what on earth she was doing there? Why she felt longing instead of fear?

She mentally shook herself. He was offering to talk. She worked her mouth into a sensible frown. She would have crossed her arms if they'd been available. "Tell me your real name."

"Ben Renfield."

"And your work?"

"What is there to tell?"

He might explain that shadow passing over his eyes. "Are you unemployed?"

"I'm on vacation."

"From?"

"From talking about work."

She tried another tactic. "What were you hunting?"

"Anything in season."

"Last I heard, the only thing in season were morels."

"Okay."

"Okay?" She tried to sit up.

He held her in place, thinking quick. It wasn't easy. His brain felt stuffed with cotton. Pain pitched and rolled up his leg. Worse, the way her body had bucked made his thoughts veer to places they rarely strayed. He felt every rise and fall as she breathed, every sculpted mound and expanse of skin. He smelled her shampoo, her soap, the tangy hint of perspiration. Wrangling on this bed, she'd glow with sweat, their bodies slick and throbbing.

She waited. The fantasy passed. "What were you hunting?" she asked flatly.

He looked into her eyes and wondered if he'd ever find it.

SIX

"You said it. Morels."

"You were hunting them," she repeated.

Ben raked his brain. He'd grown up in the Florida panhandle. What did he know of northern Michigan wildlife? He'd heard of morels; they must be common. Not that he knew what they were. Rodents? Some kind of weasel? "I thought I'd bag one for dinner."

She looked doubtful.

"Maybe two."

That seemed to convince her. She stared off at the ceiling. He breathed easier.

"You wouldn't have needed your gun," she mused. "They're pretty slow. Hard to skin too."

"I don't have a hunting knife, if that's what you're worried about. You looked through my clothes last night. And my wallet." He saw the reluctant confession in her eyes.

"Everything was in order," she admitted. "Benjamin Renfield. Age thirty-four. Weight one eighty. Credit cards. Driver's license. ID."

"No hunting license. Is that was this is about? Afraid I was poaching on your land?"

"For morels? I can honestly say the thought never entered my mind."

"Then what's the problem?"

She wriggled her arms out from under his. Touching his forehead, she played a little roughly around yesterday's welt. In fact, she poked his skull as if it were a ripe melon. "Yep, those wild morel hunters," she drawled. "Shooting off their guns at all hours. Strapping gutted morels to the roofs of their cars. There's probably a plaque in the great room downstairs, somebody's prize morel stuffed and mounted."

"Ouch."

"Too hard?"

Cattle prods were gentler. Apparently he'd strayed into another of her liberal areas. "Don't tell me you're a Bambi lover."

"I love Bambi. Dumbo too."

"Ow. I take it you don't like hunters."

She shrugged. "My philosophy is you should pick on things your own size. I mean, what did mushrooms ever do to you? Poor little defenseless fungi."

His body tensed. "Fungi?"

"It's morel *mushroom* season. That or partridge, and you didn't guess partridge." She smiled blandly up at him.

"So I lied."

"That makes—oh what, four? Five? I'm losing count." She pushed violently out from under him.

He considered keeping her where she was, talking this out. He hated lying, especially when she'd done everything to earn his gratitude. He rolled to his unhurt side and let her go, flapping the towel into place before she turned around.

He needn't have bothered. She scampered off the bed, her back to him, her arms crossed as she stared out the window.

"Bridget."

"We'll talk about this later. Somebody just drove up." She walked toward the door, deep in her own thoughts.

His heart shot into his throat. "Wait! You can't tell them I'm here."

"Why not?" She ran her hands up her arms as if a shiver had just chased up her spine.

He'd already lost her trust, her caring, her easy joy. There was no way he'd put her in danger too. "I can't tell you all of it," he confessed. "Just don't tell them I'm here." He craned toward the window. From the bed he saw only treetops.

"What are you wanted for?"

"It's not that. I'm one of the good guys. Problem is, I don't know who else is. I can't trust the cops, the hospitals, anyone. Except you. I trust you, Bridget. Promise me you won't tell anyone I'm here."

"This doesn't make much sense."

"Would you believe me if it did?"

"It'd be a first."

He took a stab at it. "I work for the government. Law enforcement. I've been keeping some people under surveillance."

"The Michigan Militia?"

"Smugglers. Drug runners, the kind who don't leave witnesses. Tell them you've seen no one."

Bridget stepped back from the window. She considered the situation for a long moment. She should have been satisfied—she'd gotten more information from him in a couple of minutes than she had all day. Unfortunately, she'd done it through trickery. The knocker boomed through the hall downstairs. "Relax. It's the mailman. I've got an express delivery coming. We'll talk about this later."

Bridget stood in the doorway. She'd climbed the stairs ready to insist he tell her more, rehearsing her get-tough attitude, only to find him out like a light. She remembered his intensity when she'd spotted the mail truck. He'd seemed more worried for her than for himself. And just wired enough to tell her the truth.

The exhaustion that claimed him minutes later wasn't surprising. Neither was the way their bodies had responded to each other. She relived it, testing her emotions. Heat fired her cheeks, matching the fever she'd felt when she lightly grazed his forehead with the backs of her fingers.

He looked troubled, even in sleep. So was she. One minute she fantasized about making love to him, the next he revealed he was an armed mushroom hunter and undercover agent. She held the package of painkillers Richie had sent. She hoped her brother hadn't scrimped on his own for a man he'd never met. "Must run in the family."

She left his lunch on a tray. A pill and a note sat beside the glass of juice. For the time being, sleep was better for him than pills. She gently combed the hair off his forehead, grazing his skin again for signs of fever.

She almost felt sorry for him. The poor man was

caught between a rocky cliff and a very deep lake. She had no intention of betraying him, but she wasn't about to let him go until he told her who, what, where, and why. The minute he woke up she'd demand answers.

What time was it? The light was nearly gone. In early summer that meant nine, nine-thirty. Had he slept that long?

He sat up, swaying with wooziness. He pushed the tray away, noting the pill he'd refused to take. She'd stopped by late in the afternoon. He remembered arguing, something about not taking any damn drugs from strangers.

He winced and scraped a hand over the back of his neck. He'd hurt her feelings, calling her a stranger. No time to worry about that. He'd spent a day out of commission. He had to find that telephone if it killed him.

He staggered to his feet, every muscle in his body reminding him of his aborted trek earlier that afternoon. He remembered his body on hers, the feel of skin against skin. He'd probably dreamed that part while losing the rest of the day to sleep.

At least the clothes were real. She'd brought them her second visit. Grasping a fistful, he leaned back against the bed. He didn't bother with underwear. With a leg that wouldn't bend, getting pants on was difficult enough. Thanks to the 1920s style, the slacks were pleated flannel and wide as clown pants. It helped.

The old-fashioned T-shirt mimicked a muscle shirt, scooping halfway to his nipples. He slung a cotton shirt over his shoulders, not bothering with buttons. The whole getup smelled of the cedar closet she'd pulled it from. He felt stronger already.

The stairs were manageable. The hand-hewn rail's irregular surface rippled beneath his palm. No more searching endless bedrooms; he'd head straight for the kitchen.

And if she saw him? "Sorry, sweetheart. Nothing stops me this time." She'd probably smell him first.

Sweat poured freely down his chest. He ignored it. He couldn't be tapped out so fast. He mentally mapped out a route down the hall and past the great room. Large tables lined the walls, topped with trophies and hunting-lodge paraphernalia. Two small lamps were lit to dispel the gloom. The chandeliers hung dark.

Using the log walls for support, he slid an old walking stick from a copper umbrella stand for insurance.

Blue-and-white light flickered from a slit in the great-room doors. She was probably in there watching TV. Barefoot, he'd sneak right by.

Raised voices stopped him dead. Men's voices. He strained to hear. Melodramatic music from the television nearly drowned them out. A woman's strangled plea made the blood back up in his veins.

They'd found her.

Everything came into razor-sharp focus. They'd traced him, gotten in. He didn't know what she'd told them; he only knew he hadn't told her enough. He'd gotten her into this; he had to save her.

He clutched the cane. He had no advantage except surprise. If she hadn't told them he was there, he might catch them off guard.

He limped two steps and tore an antique rifle from its wall display. Remembering the spitfire of their semiautomatics in the woods, he figured he just might get the drop on them with the old Winchester. As long as they didn't laugh themselves sick first.

Sweat trickled in his eye. Dizziness washed over him. Tough. He took a deep breath and slid the door open an inch. The angle wasn't good. He glimpsed a corner of the roaring fire, heard another strangled cry, and knew in his gut he couldn't wait another minute, not when he heard the way one man laughed, or the way she whimpered when her blouse tore.

He slammed the log door open, his shout hoarse and ugly, the rifle raised. "Let her go! Now! Freeze, you—"

Bridget's scream rent the air. She leaped off the couch, popcorn flying everywhere. With the afghan wound around her, mummy-style, she tottered, screamed again, and landed butt-first on the floor. Considering the madman who'd just invaded her movie, it wasn't such a bad place to be.

A stunned silence descended over the room. She peeked over the sofa arm. Ben stood planted in the doorway, legs spread, jaw set. "What the heck are you doing?" she asked very, very softly.

He strafed the room with a glance. The gun barrel followed his gaze. If it hadn't been for the disheveled hair and black stubble, she might not have recognized him. The clothes were loose and flapping. The man inside them was hard as iron. Eyes black with fury, he looked like John Wayne and Sylvester Stallone rolled into one.

He continued searching, looking in every corner, scanning the hem of every curtain. White kernels littered the floor. The whites of her eyes probably matched them.

"You're okay," he concluded.

"May I ask what the hell you're doing?" she replied as reasonably as she could.

He lowered the rifle, keeping his finger near the trigger. "I heard voices. I thought you were in danger."

"I was watching a movie."

"I told you not to let anyone in."

"Not even Humphrey Bogart?" She gathered her empty popcorn bowl to her chest. Grabbing the remote, she muted the movie. "I thought you were asleep."

"I woke up."

He certainly had. He looked drawn but alert. Adrenaline pumped through him. His body glistened. He'd be any woman's idea of a hero. Except this woman wasn't in distress—unless she counted the way she reacted to the sight of him.

"Did you take that pill?" she asked lamely. Power such as he had displayed didn't come from any pain pill.

He set the gun on a table and limped to the sofa. Crisis passed, the energy faded fast. He nodded at the television. "If the smugglers *were* looking for me, that could have been you."

"It's true, then? The government-agent stuff?" She sat beside him, her hand instantly going to his forehead.

His troubled gaze rested on hers a long moment. A log spat an ember onto the hearth. "It's not a dream, Bridget. And it's no hallucination."

Funny, it felt like one. He'd come in the room ready to fight for her with all he had.

"I wouldn't let anyone hurt you. But there's only so much I can do without your help. You could be in danger with me here."

"You're serious about the smugglers."

"Is this serious?" He laid her hand on his thigh, just below where the wine-dark spot seeped through the flannel.

She recalled the jagged tear in his skin. Her stomach lurched at the thought of someone deliberately shooting him. "You'll need another bandage."

"First I need that telephone. Please."

"You'll never make it to the kitchen."

"Then help me." His tone warned her he'd find it with or without her help. The pale cast to his cheeks told her he'd collapse trying.

"Take a painkiller first," she parried.

"No. I need to be alert."

"Then I'll make the call," she said. "You said it yourself, there's no reason I should trust you. How do I know you're not one of the smugglers? Maybe they shot you because a deal went down wrong."

He cracked a smile at her idea of gangster lingo. "I'll give you the number. It's a government agency. You won't recognize the name."

"What should I tell them?"

"Don't worry. They'll do all the asking."

Sitting at the kitchen table, Bridget took a steadying breath. She'd put him to bed on the sofa. She would rebandage his leg when she went back in. That meant getting him out of his clothes.

She clutched the receiver, studying the number she'd scribbled down. She'd trusted him from the first. The lie about morel hunting had nearly destroyed that trust. His delirious attempt to rescue her had brought it all rushing back. Was she a gullible fool?

She thought of the people she'd met in San Francisco. When someone was hurting you didn't ask why, you helped.

She dialed.

Coffee table behind her, sofa in front, she knelt in the narrow space and bandaged Ben's extended leg. He hugged the discarded slacks over his lap, the afghan atop them.

"I know I set out a pair of boxers," she muttered, the end of a clean bandage clamped between her teeth as she unrolled another strip.

"I didn't have time to put them on."

She dropped the bandage in distaste as she cut away the blood-soaked original. "In that much of a hurry to save me?"

He grunted. "Did you make the call?"

"Typical bureaucracy. Endless voice mail and no human being at the other end. I'll have to try tomorrow."

He nodded, temporarily satisfied.

Bridget had been afraid of disappointing him. Her gaze fell to the roll of bandages in her hand. She held on to her heart as he raised her face to his. "Sorry to scare you."

"I thought you'd gone nuts."

"Better to err on the side of caution. I had to know

you were safe." It meant a lot to him. It was the third time he'd tried to explain.

Bridget concentrated on her nursing.

"I'm making a mess of your life," he said.

"Then tell me what you do with yours."

"I handle anything that crosses borders. Smuggling between here and Canada would involve customs, the DEA, the ATF, the RCMP—the Mounties. Even the FBI, if they smuggle anything from Michigan to Wisconsin. Not to mention local police and sheriff's departments. To keep them all from stepping on each other's toes, I get called in."

"Just you?" She snipped the bandage and tied it off.

"I've got backup. Deep back. I work alone as much as I can. Then I let them know who we'll need from which agency."

"And who you can trust."

He touched her again. She wished he wouldn't. Her hands shook as she tied the knot; he had to notice.

He was too busy staring into her eyes. "All that matters to me is that the right thing gets done. Not the red tape, not the collar. I don't need the recognition."

"Or anyone else?"

He looked down, flexing the muscle in his leg as if testing how much pain he could take. "It's a good job for me. I'm good at working alone."

"And living alone?"

"Yeah. Not that I'm proud of it."

"Being single is nothing to be ashamed of."

"It is if you failed your family." He shook his head, searching the dark corners of the cavernous room for something he'd lost, looking for another way to explain it. "I wasn't a very good husband."

"I have trouble believing that," she scolded softly.

"Then you haven't met my ex-wife."

She grinned because he did. "Why?"

"Carla said I was useless, not a very faithful husband."

"You? I'd have never guessed. Not after the way you burst in here to save me. Still, working in remote places the way you do, you might get lonely, meet a woman."

"Like now?"

She paused.

He shook his head impatiently. "It wasn't that. I was never around. Most men think they'll settle down once they meet a woman. I meant to work less, to put in for a desk job. But after the baby, work seemed more important than ever. I needed to protect them, make the world a safer place. Crime, life and death, it all seemed more urgent than which day-care center we'd send Molly to or why Carla's mother had gotten on her nerves that day."

Bridget had heard similar stories from stressed-out executives. "Work becomes more urgent than the people it's meant to support."

"But it's *for* them." He sighed. "If you love somebody, you'd do anything to make it a safer world for them."

Bridget pondered that. "Tell me about her, your daughter."

"Molly?"

"How old is she?"

"Six. I haven't seen her in four years."

"Ben! Four years?"

"She has a new father. I figured if I couldn't be the kind of father I wanted to be, I'd let someone else have a try. I'll stick with what I do best."

She studied him a long time. "Tell me about when she was born."

"That's right, you're interested in babies."

She shot him a wry smile. "Let's not start that again. I'm more than a ticking biological clock."

"I thought the alarm was set to go off in nine months?"

"Eight if everything works out. So? Her birthday."

Reflected flames couldn't outshimmer the faraway look in his eyes. "It was the greatest day of my life. This little life, and she was all mine. I swore I'd work night and day to keep her safe."

"But Carla didn't want you working night and day," she suggested.

"No. I can't commute to a desk every morning. That's not the way this job works. I couldn't convince her of that."

"Where are they now?"

"On the other side of the country."

"And you?"

"Anywhere my work takes me. Borders. Coast-lines, mostly."

"Why don't you visit them? Next time you're on their coast?"

"I don't want to disrupt her life."

"And yours? Don't you rate a visit with your daughter?"

"Getting philosophical?"

"While you're out saving the world, who cares for you?"

"I can take care of myself."

She shook her head. "Everybody needs some-body."

The fist in his lap had become an open palm. She'd have reached for it if it hadn't rested in the juncture of his thighs. She twined her fingers, sensing his shoulder close to hers.

"Who do you have?" he countered.

"I've got Richie. My parents."

He made a show of looking around. "I don't see 'em."

"I needed to sort things out on my own. Gestate."

"Right. The baby."

"I knew life wasn't turning out the way I'd envisioned it, with a husband and family. When Richie got sick I decided to stop waiting for life to live up to my expectations. Better to deal with what is than what should be."

"So you gave up on getting married."

"It could still happen. It will. Just not in one-two-three fashion."

"And not anytime soon."

"No one on the horizon."

They watched the fire as if it were a distant horizon.

"What did you think when life brought you me?" he asked.

She laughed wickedly. "I thought the cosmos was playing a very cruel joke."

He chuckled with her. Hitching a breath, he lifted his arm and laid it across the back of the sofa. She sat very still, their faces level.

"Why are you shaking your head?" she asked.

"Because you're too beautiful to have a baby alone."

"Now, there's a line I haven't heard."

"Hard to imagine life messing up so badly."

"Hard to imagine you were a bad husband."

"Have you been imagining?"

"I haven't had a lot of facts to work with."

"Sorry about the lies." His voice rustled low. "You're too beautiful to live alone." He reached up, lifting her chin with his thumb. The logs crackled. His lips brushed hers.

SEVEN

"It's okay," he murmured. "I wanted to know if this afternoon was a dream."

"Which part?"

"Us together. On a bed."

"You fell," she said quickly.

"You stayed."

"You were worn-out."

"Not too worn-out to know I had a woman under me."

She shrugged as if it didn't matter. Her shoulder grazed his. "An automatic physical response," she said. "I didn't take it seriously."

"I did. What about my offer?"

"Which one was that?"

"You need a man to have a baby."

Her gaze grew ultra-tolerant. "Uh, let me explain the science one more time."

"You said it might not take."

"In which case you're volunteering?" She looked skyward. "God grant me a Boy Scout every time."

"It's an offer."

"You're recuperating. You might give it time."

"Usually I do." He fingered her hair. "So why does this feel so natural so soon?"

"Sometimes there are sparks—" She glanced at the fire to prove her point. "Light a match to any wood, and it will burn."

"We're any man and woman, is that it?"

"Could be."

He kissed her again, proving her all wrong.

She couldn't remember the last time she'd felt her heart beat. She'd thought it was errant chemistry between them, a good-looking man, a woman who always cared more than she let on . . . but she'd been mistaken.

He pressed her softly back, supporting her head with his arm. His biceps flexed, raising her face a scant inch. He tasted good, patient. Crooking his arm alongside her neck, he rasped the cotton sleeve against her sensitive skin. He couldn't know how good that felt, and wouldn't ever have known except for the mew that escaped her throat. She blushed at how vulnerable she sounded, how willing.

"Ben?" She touched his face. She meant to stop him, to cup his cheek in a firm, dignified way and look him in the eye and tell him what was happening made no sense. It would never work. She hardly knew him.

Her gaze got no higher than his lips. She knew he was alone, that he clung to a solitary way of life the way the lodge clung to its rocky perch.

His tongue skimmed his upper lip. Hers darted out to meet it. She'd die if she didn't taste him one more time.

He was like velvet, wet and slick and pulsing.

Boldness was a fundamental part of him, a frank eroticism that expected no less from her. She quivered as he coaxed her tongue into his mouth with suggestive strokes.

Her sagging willpower told her to stop. Her conscience told her her actions weren't wise. Her body ignored their well-meaning advice. Life didn't follow rules. It cared nothing for sense, for one-two-three and romantic do's and don'ts.

Every inch of her body shimmered. Thrills of excitement chased through her. She was hungry, and she wasn't about to ask Why now or How long will it last? The moment could escape right then if she didn't capture it with both hands.

She began to speak. Her voice failed, tripped up by his tenderness. He held her as if she'd break, as if he would. He slid his hand beneath her sweater, his palm stealing warmth from her silk, returning it. His thumb brushed her nipple.

She'd known they were taut. She never guessed how sensitive. He filled both his hands, and she melted. Her face grazed the side of his neck, her lips tracing the sinewy cords, her teeth nipping.

She wriggled closer. He fitted his hands to her waist and hauled her closer. Her knee thudded his thigh. His gasp cut off a curse.

She snapped out of her spell. "Oh my God. Are you all right?"

He held up a palm, waiting for the pain to pass.

"Ben, I'm sorry."

He leveled a tortured look her way, his eyes black in the firelight. "I'm not. I don't know what the hell I was doing. Maybe it's better this way."

Maybe. She scampered off the sofa, a draft from

somewhere chilling her. She certainly didn't want to throw herself at him. If he didn't want this— "I, uh, let me get you another pillow."

"I'm fine."

"A quilt. It could get cold if the fire goes out."

"Bridget."

She turned from the hearth where she'd been stabbing the embers with a poker.

"This fire isn't going out," he said levelly. "And I don't need a pillow."

Another draft whispered across her, carrying his scent from where it clung to her skin, cedar and musk. She nervously swallowed the taste of his tongue on hers. Slinging a strand of hair behind one ear, she then fluffed her bangs and crossed her arms securely across her front. "We got kind of carried away there."

Ben nodded. Inside he cursed. She looked so shook up, and she was trying so hard to cover it with a cocky I-can-handle-it attitude. It was nothing, her posture seemed to say. Horsefeathers.

Even if he could trust his leg to support him, lurching across the carpet to take her in his arms wouldn't be suave in anybody's book. Chasing her was out of the question. Nevertheless, he ached to kiss the doubt off her downturned mouth, to ease those folded arms back around his neck. "I'm not husband material."

Her jaw dropped. "I wasn't exactly proposing!"

"I meant I can't offer you anything. It's not as if I could take you anywhere—on a date, to meet the folks. Maybe it's better we stopped when we did."

She turned back to the fire, her face outlined by orange flame. Apparently she had her own opinion on that subject. She kept it to herself.

"I wanted to thank you," he rasped out.

"Does that include—" She stopped midsentence, drawing up the collar of her sweater as if the silky chemise itched against her skin. "If that's 'thanks' I'd hate to see 'you're welcome.' Tell you what, I'll get you another pillow."

"No, dammit!"

She froze.

He punched the two she'd already brought, shoving them into place against the sofa arm. "I thought you needed somebody. I wanted to repay you. You've been a great help." He winced. A thank-you note to his great-aunt Gilda wasn't the style he was reaching for. "I've wanted to touch you ever since I woke up this afternoon and remembered you underneath me. Did you know that?"

"Consider your curiosity quenched."

He shook his head. Frostiness was no defense. "I wasn't doing this alone, Bridget."

Her cheeks glowed hot pink. He waited her out.

"Maybe you need someone more than you think," she said cautiously.

Her sincerity humbled him. Being there for a woman was a test he'd already flunked. He clamped his hands behind his head and lay back, eyes fixed on the beamed ceiling. "What I need is a telephone and a way out of here. I'll handle the rest myself."

To his consternation and secret relief, she didn't fold up and slink away. She was stronger than that, more resilient. Pacing the length of the massive hearth, she turned on her heel and planted herself right in front of him.

"You think you know what I need?"

He kept a smart-ass reply to himself. "I might."

She closed her eyes and breathed deep. "What I really want—" A sensual smile played across her full lips. Her lids fluttered.

His gut grew tighter than a miser's fist. "What do you want?"

She exhaled long and slow. "A cigarette."

His tension eased. Slightly. "A cigarette?"

She swung her hands wide. "I'm an addict. What did you expect? Besides, I could really use one right now." She rubbed her arms briskly.

He knew how she felt. That kiss had affected both of them.

"Just one." She sighed. "One perfect pack."

"One pack is twenty cigarettes."

"I'd *buy* one pack. Then I'd open it. I'd listen to the crinkle of cellophane. Feel the crackle of it in my hand. Sniff it. Tobacco smells so great fresh out of the pack."

"And stinks so bad in an ashtray."

"Are you saying you wouldn't kiss me if I tasted like cigarettes?"

The look they traded sizzled hotter than the fire. "I'd have to find out."

"Unh-unh." She shook her head, her hair whispering over her shoulders. "You'll never find out if I never backslide."

He pictured her on her back, her hair spread on a pillow. She'd slide across the sheets as his body filled her.

"On the other hand, who says I can't fantasize once in a while?"

"Fantasies can get you in trouble." His raspy voice and throbbing body testified to that.

She tilted her head to one side, sticking to the

safety of this particular daydream. "I'd slide one from the pack. Real slow. It'd be long, thin, white, the paper smooth in my hands, the tobacco rustling softly inside it. I'd crumple the rest of the pack and throw it away. Really. Just like that. I only need one."

Not him. He'd already pictured their next kiss. And the one after that. And the sweaty, driving, exhaustive lovemaking session they'd share.

"I'd strike a match."

He was on fire.

"Then I'd put the cigarette to my lips." She pursed them, sucking softly. "The flame would jump—"

The way his pulse jumped.

"I'd inhale. That first wonderful drag would fill my mouth, the smoke curling down into my lungs."

"Your blackened lungs," he muttered.

She waved him off like a curlicue of smoke. Shoulders high, breasts rising, she drew in a long, satisfied breath. "I'd smoke it right down to the filter. Then I'd tap off the ashes and snuff it out. Good-bye, cigarette."

"Until the next time."

She slowly opened her eyes. "Do you think I'm that weak?"

"Nicotine's more addictive than heroin." And sex had been known to turn strong men against everything they believed.

"Luckily there are few things more life changing than babies."

"Babies?"

"Getting pregnant is the best motivator to quit that I know of. When I'm sure I'm pregnant, it'll be easy."

If that didn't cool his ardor, what would? The throbbing ebbed. He cleared his throat and his conscience. "You can quit anything if you put your mind to it. It's a question of willpower."

"And priorities."

His job was his biggest priority. For years it had been his only one.

She laughed. "Of course, it helps that the closest cigarettes are at the general store in Lac LaBelle. Oh well. Four days and counting. See you in the morning." She breezed out of the room.

" 'Night," he said.

Four days? He'd been there twenty-four hours and he was falling apart. After one full day she had him questioning what mattered most in his world. Was it about catching criminals? Or the people one fought the criminals to protect? He'd stormed in here ready to die trying. All for her.

Fantasies. Dreams. He set himself straight. The number she'd called was a fake designed for agents in trouble. The endless messages were a ruse to give the agency time to trace the line. It was only a matter of time before they came to pick him up. Why not leave it at that? No more temptation, no more chipper good mornings or frowns of concern as she changed his bandages or slid a cool washcloth over his chest.

He grunted and rolled onto his good side. He'd be gone by tomorrow. And she'd be alone, working on this big old lodge, turning it into a spa for stressed-out execs who could pick and choose their vacations. He'd stumbled on her by accident, a lifesaver found floating on the sea, a light in the darkness, a lamp in the window.

He scanned the room, thinking about the wolves

who lurked in that forest, the kind who carried guns and trafficked in things more addictive than nicotine.

"If there is such a thing," he muttered. A grim smile creased his mouth at her uninhibited reenactment of the sheer sensual pleasure of smoking. She was stronger than she knew. He'd have to be equally strong to forget her.

She was funny, sweet, candid, unconscionably sexy. He'd won her trust more than earned it, like a lottery he'd never expected to win.

He punched his pillow and stared at the dying flames. Leave that ticket where it lay. When it came to women, fantasies were all he dared claim.

Bridget swung the big door open before the elderly man could lift the knocker. "Hello."

For a stranger on her doorstep he took the surprise with benign calm. His white hair glistened in the morning light. Combed straight back off his high forehead, the style emphasized his aquiline nose. He wore a bow tie, a tan summer suit, and carried a weathered briefcase at his side. A befuddled, absentminded professor if she ever saw one.

Nevertheless, Bridget remembered Ben's warning about visitors. She had just helped him upstairs from the great room when she'd heard footsteps on the front porch.

The elderly gentleman pulled a handkerchief from his breast pocket and dabbed his forehead. "I'm so sorry to intrude, but I've had a spot of car trouble."

She listened to her intuition. He didn't seem dangerous.

"You know, I couldn't recall the rule regarding

disabled vehicles. Does one stay with the car or go for help?"

"Way out here you could wait quite awhile before a car came along."

"And if one waits, one might be eaten by a bear?"

"Hardly a daily occurrence." She laughed. A smuggler? She'd bet the Jeep this man had never smuggled anything more serious than dusty textbooks or Greek friezes. "We're four miles from the blacktop. I'm surprised you found us."

"Was it that far?" He dabbed once more and returned the handkerchief to his pocket. "Although to tell you the truth, this was my intended goal. This is the Dodge residence, is it not?"

"How did you know?"

"Excuse me, my name's Stonesmith. Carville Stonesmith. I was an executive with General Motors for many years, the last few in the archives department. I visited Henry Ford's Huron Mountain Club the day before yesterday. Today I was hoping to find the Dodges' answer to it." He balanced his bifocals on his nose, taking in everything he could spy from the porch.

Bridget grinned. "Would you like a tour?"

"Would you mind?"

Well versed in the history of the major automotive families, her visitor dropped names and dates casually into the conversation. Half an hour later they paused in the kitchen. "I'm so sorry," Bridget declared. "It's been so long since I've had someone to talk to, I'm really bending your ear."

"Are you here alone?"

She sidestepped the question. "You'll have to excuse me for running on. I should have asked earlier if you'd like something to drink."

"My dear, I enjoyed every minute of your tour, and I'd enjoy a lemonade almost as much."

She smiled and poured him one.

"Not that I wish to distract you from your work, but you mentioned twenty bedrooms?"

"Upstairs. All in different stages of remodeling. We're keeping the downstairs as original as possible."

"Would you mind if I—"

"I'm afraid it's a mess up there."

"I promise to keep my eyes closed. It was the facilities I was inquiring about."

"Ah, the bathroom." Where were her manners? She directed him to the back staircase. "They're kind of steep. From here the bathroom will be the third door on your right."

"Thank you."

Uneasy, she paused at the foot of the stairs as he went up. Ben's suspicious nature was rubbing off on her. She couldn't very well shadow the man to the bathroom door, then stand guard outside like a sentry.

Clamping her hands behind her back, she paced to the refrigerator for a carrot stick she didn't want. Nerves. Nicotine withdrawal.

Or instinct?

He'd taken his briefcase. Did he distrust *her*? Or was he assembling some complicated deadly weapon out of its red velvet interior? She rolled her eyes. That didn't prevent her edging back to the foot of the stairs. She sneaked up them, poking her head into the empty hall. The bathroom door was shut, the water running.

Scolding herself for unwarranted paranoia, she retreated to the kitchen. One step into the room, she froze. A cigarette pack lay on the table, its cellophane shiny in the morning light. Why hadn't she noticed it before? She looked closer. One filter poked suggestively out of the open end.

Her heart quickened. He must have left it. The delicious fragrance wafted toward her, barely detectable. It was a new pack, nearly full. Surely he wouldn't notice if one were missing.

She clamped her hand over her mouth. "Oh no, you don't."

Stonesmith slapped the leather briefcase onto the bed.

"Watch the leg," Ben muttered.

"Isn't it a little late for you to be warning *me*?" Stonesmith settled the stethoscope's prongs in his ears and leaned forward. "Inhale."

"I've got a broken rib."

The distinguished retiree scowled. "Inhale."

Ben did his best. He felt the bandages grip and chased away the memory of Bridget's arms around him as she'd helped him up the stairs. He was back in "his" bedroom. "So how're you getting me out of here? What's the story?"

"I don't know," Stonesmith murmured. He fit the stethoscope in his briefcase, retrieving a pair of scissors. "Which leg?"

"The one with the bandage on it." Ben flipped the bedspread up. Having slept in flannel slacks downstairs on the sofa, it had been a relief stripping to the boxers in bed.

Stonesmith snipped the bandage off. "Wound looks clean."

"She bandaged it last night." She'd taken a lot of care. Ben watched her work discarded in a pile beside the bed.

"Ugly path. Nine-millimeter?"

"That was my guess."

"You'll have scar tissue. I won't have to amputate."

"As Dr. Mudd said to John Wilkes Booth."

"Shoot any presidents lately?"

"Only an agency doctor who wouldn't tell me what's up."

"By the way, where is your gun?"

"I dropped it. I told them that." He'd waited an hour after Bridget had left him in the great room for the night. Limping to the kitchen, he'd found the telephone and made a call of his own.

"Just checking," Stonesmith replied. "You carry a forty-five, I believe?" He handed one over.

"Got any painkillers in that little black bag?"

"A year's supply." Stonesmith slapped a white square of cotton on Ben's thigh and proceeded to re-bandage the leg. "But I see you have your own."

He hadn't wanted to draw attention to the dresser. "You never even looked that way."

"Training. I'm sure your instincts are equally sharp."

Rusty and dull was more like it. He felt like some rookie who had to be airlifted out because he'd screwed up. Worse, he already missed Bridget. He hated the idea of disappearing on her without a good-bye.

"She seems very nice."

"She's fine," he replied, keeping his tone neutral.

"Not at all suspicious?"

"She let you in, didn't she?"

"I'm supremely trustworthy, you know that."

"It's that eastern-seaboard old-school-tie act."

"Does she trust you?"

"She thinks I can't tell the time of day without bending the truth."

"Ah. She's caught you, then."

"More than once."

"Must be slipping."

"Hazard of the trade."

"Or a very perceptive woman."

"So what am I going to do?"

"Be honest with her?"

"Thank you, Dear Abby. I meant, am I tied to a desk for the rest of this operation, or are they letting me back in the field?"

Stonesmith pursed his lips, fussing to get the bandage knot just right. "It will be a while before you heal. As you said yourself, there's no telling what kind of look the smugglers got at you. Do you think they're on your trail?"

"I thought you could plant an item in the *Mining Gazette*."

"Saying?"

"Hunter found dead. Accidental gunshot. That oughta end any search."

"Consider it done."

Ben breathed a sigh of relief as Stonesmith put his doctor tools away. The older man sauntered to the dresser. "By the way, where'd she get the pills?"

A chill crept up Ben's spine. He blamed it on the scent of raw alcohol. Snatching a soaked gauze pad from Stonesmith's hand, he dabbed his own scratches. "I've been wondering that myself."

"Does she need them?"

For morning sickness? He doubted it. Just as he doubted Stonesmith would drop the subject.

"Possession of illegally prescribed drugs," Stonesmith murmured, reading the label. "We might gain her cooperation with this."

"She's already cooperated. If she stepped over the line, it was strictly to help me."

"A judge might not see it that way."

"The whole thing would be tossed out as entrapment. A bleeding man shows up on her doorstep, asks for help, what's she supposed to do?"

"Steady, steady. Methinks thou doth protect the lady too much. Do you think she'll talk about you when you're gone?"

To whom? She was alone. Her closest friend seemed to be her brother, and he was dying. "She won't say anything if I ask her not to."

That meant he'd need a few minutes with her. He'd get his chance to say good-bye.

Stonesmith considered his statement. "I'll think about it."

Bridget held the slim white cylinder in her hand. The paper was smooth and cool, just as she'd envisioned. The tobacco rustled as she rolled it between her thumb and index finger.

She glared at the ceiling. Why couldn't he have been a pipe smoker? She had a baby to think about. Maybe. The insemination might not have worked. Ergo, it might not hurt to have just one.

Like a kiss? She closed her eyes and drew the filter across her lips. The smell reminded her of the woodpile beside the fireplace, which reminded her of Ben.

She remembered the way she'd substituted her desire for a cigarette for her desire for him. Karma, that's what it was. "One weak wish and temptation shows up on my doorstep."

Actually, temptation was ensconced in a bedroom upstairs, waiting for her to clear away his breakfast tray. After the previous night she'd thought it wise not to sit with him while he ate. She'd spent ten minutes vacuuming popcorn kernels from the rug downstairs instead.

She laughed to herself, recalling the way he'd burst into the room to save her from intruders.

Her heart nearly stopped. He'd risked his life to save her, and what did she do? She went and let a stranger in the front door!

"He can't be dangerous."

But would she bet Ben's life on it?

She crumpled the cigarette and raced for the stairs. Who knew what smugglers looked like? Who knew how many rooms he'd had a chance to poke his nose into by now? That damn cigarette hadn't shortened her life, but it sure as hell had put Ben's on the line.

Feet pounding the stairs, she cleared the top and burst into the hallway.

Mr. Carville Stonesmith emerged from the bathroom. "Wonderful old place. The plumbing, is that pure copper? Mined right here at Copper Harbor, I wouldn't be surprised. But my dear, you're panting."

EIGHT

"Where is he?" Bridget wasn't buying the sweet-old-gentleman act. She raced down the hall. Ben sat up as the door slammed open. His shirt half on, he swung his legs over the side of the bed.

Bridget ran to him. A warning in his eyes stopped her from throwing her arms around his neck. Her fists clenched at her sides, her heart thudded in her chest. "You're all right."

"For now," Stonesmith commented behind her.

She swung around, placing herself between Ben and a stranger who obviously knew more than he pretended.

"You've taken very good care of him," the old man said smoothly.

"Who are you?"

"A friend."

She wasn't moving.

"A colleague. Should we tell her the plan, Benjamin?"

"As soon as you tell it to me." Ben glowered as

Stonesmith strolled to the side table. The older man rolled a light yellow pill between his fingers.

"She's on our side," Ben said with a growl.

"It's my fondest hope she'll stay that way."

"What the hell do you mean?"

Bridget looked from one man to the other. Her gaze rested on Ben the longest. From the way they spoke, Ben didn't seem to be in any danger. She had the creepy-crawly sensation she was. "Would either one of you care to let me in on this?"

"I will as soon as I know," Ben replied. "What've you got up your sleeve this time, Carville?"

"A very simple plan. However, before I introduce myself, I'd like to tell our hostess a little of the background we've discovered about her. We've done our homework."

Minutes later Bridget curled her hand around the bedframe. The extent of their knowledge made her blood run colder than the brittle iron. Stonesmith seemed to know everything about her, from her birth date to her last job rating. She'd half expected him to drop in the name of the insemination clinic. He'd spared her that. Not that she was ashamed; she refused to be ashamed of wanting to bring a life into this world. She just wasn't used to being so . . . exposed. "What are you, CIA?"

Stonesmith chuckled. "We work across all conventional law-enforcement lines. That gives us rather broad access to information. For instance, the U.S. mail."

"Nobody tampers with the mail. My dad was a mailman, I know."

"Then you know it's illegal to mail drugs across state lines?"

She kept her gaze on his when it would have darted elsewhere.

Ben stood, hissing in pain at the sudden movement. He gripped her shoulders from behind. Bridget stood like a rock; she thought he needed the support. When she felt his fingers flex along her collarbone she realized *he* was the one offering. The sweetness of it nearly buckled her knees.

"That's enough, Carville," he growled out. "I said no threats."

Bridget eased out from under his hands. Chin raised, she stepped up to Mr. Stonesmith. She kept her voice deliberately level. "You leave my brother out of this."

"He mailed a drug across state lines. Quite a potent one."

"To help one of your agents."

"He didn't know that at the time."

"Why, you—"

"Ms. Bernard, are you prepared to help us?"

"She already has," Ben said in disgust.

"What I'm asking will require a longer commitment than these past few days. I'd like you to allow Mr. Renfield to stay."

"What?" Ben exploded.

"Stay?" Bridget whispered. She sank onto the bed, barely hearing Stonesmith's next words.

"You have a perfect location for observing the traffic on the lake night and day. I trust a few people know you're here?"

"I haven't made any secret of it."

"Good. Then no one will be startled to see a light in the window or a car going back and forth. However, no one must know Mr. Renfield is here. You'll need to be very careful whom you talk to and what you say."

Bridget looked their gentleman caller up and down. She felt foolishly fragile, as if her body were made of clay. Nothing seemed real anymore, including the totally uncalled-for sensation threading through her veins, a gleeful whisper, repeating the word *stay*.

She squelched the yearning with a hard dose of reality. None of this had been what it seemed, not their kiss, not Carville's "forgotten" cigarettes. She'd remember that the next time she was tempted to open her heart to Mr. Ben Renfield.

He moved toward her as she hesitated. She shook her head. He held back.

"Will you help us?" Stonesmith asked. "And more importantly, will you promise to tell no one?"

"Believe me," she croaked, "I won't make the mistake of trusting anyone again."

"Then if you'll excuse us, I have some details I need to work out with my agent."

"Be my guest." She walked stiffly from the room.

"I'm sorry."

Bridget shrugged, tucking the sheets into the mattress. "It didn't look like you had much say in it."

The afternoon was waning, and she'd gotten no work done. Moving Ben from the first bedroom to the master corner suite had taken nearly two hours. She'd gotten him fresh towels for the bathroom and another set of clothes from the storage closets. He'd barely noticed. Slinging on a beige pair of 1920s flannels, he hadn't even bothered with the suspenders. They dangled by his thighs as he peered through his state-of-the-art telescope.

Personally Bridget had never found the low-slung-oversized-jeans look attractive. A teenage fad designed to drive parents to despair, she thought. Baggy worked on Ben. What wouldn't? His broad, bare shoulders were eye-catching, to say the least. The wide swath of bandage around his ribs did nothing to minimize the slimness of his waist. The sagging slacks on his narrow hips emphasized the hardness and sculpted discipline of the body inside, not to mention the white elastic band of the silk boxers. Those fit if nothing else did.

She pictured him in nothing else. "Ow!"

"You okay?"

She hopped on the toe she'd stubbed. "Whoever came up with the idea of giving beds legs?"

He frowned and went back to his telescope. "I can see every mile of shoreline from Keweenaw Point to Bête Grise lighthouse. If I'd known you had such a vantage point, I'd have been in here sooner."

"Why would I let you in my bedroom?"

Hers? Ben twisted around. Not a good idea with bruised ribs. Bridget saw the grimace before averting her own gaze. Bruised toes and broken ribs. Some pair they made.

She stuffed in another sheet end. It still wasn't taut enough for her taste. Her nerves were another matter.

Tearing his gaze from her, Ben scanned the golden walls and one surface of aged wallpaper. He noted the fringed lampshades from the flapper era, the muslin drapes she'd slung from an utterly feminine four-poster. A pastel Oriental rug covered the polished wood floor between two painted dressers with stenciled vines.

The bed canted away from the wall at an angle, the better to offset the square shape of the tower. A person could lie there and watch the lake from windows on three sides. Her room. Why hadn't he noticed before? Wildflowers sat in vases on the sills above the window seat. The scent hovering in the air was unmistakably hers.

"Did you move the bed by yourself?"

She shrugged. "It doesn't weigh that much with the mattress off."

"In your condition—"

"My condition's fine, thank you. I couldn't resist the view." She nodded at the central windows. "Due east. Can't get a better wake-up call than that."

"Where will you be waking up tomorrow?"

They both ignored the implications of that question. "Next door down. Same view, no tower."

"No lights after midnight. No change in your routine."

"Yes, Mr. Stonesmith. I got my instructions."

They stood on either side of the bed, staring foolishly at the stiff sheets. She could've bounced a quarter off them.

"Need anything else?" He was a guest, her tone implied. An assignment. She'd been recruited; that meant they were on official terms. The government, in the person of one Mr. Ben Renfield, had commandeered room and board. However long it lasted, this visit would not be marred by unchecked desires or illogical longings. She had a job to do. So did he.

"Anything else?" she asked briskly.

For a fleeting second a shadow passed across his features like a cloud scudding across the lake. He turned toward the square tower and scraped an armchair into place. His hand dawdled over notepads, a calendar, lake maps, and land maps. He rattled the handful of pencils she'd fetched for him.

"I didn't think I'd be staying."

"It didn't sound as if you wanted to."

It hurt to realize she'd been right. That's what she was feeling, Bridget decided, hurt. Not desire, not the awkwardness of two people finding themselves alone at last. It was plain old hurt that had her avoiding his every look, bustling around the lodge like she had a hundred guests coming for the weekend instead of one.

She'd been so frightened, so sure she'd done something stupid by letting Stonesmith in the house. Every protective instinct she'd had kicked in when she'd run to Ben's room. Even when she'd found them in league, it hadn't quenched that tiny flash of irrational hope when she'd heard the word *stay*.

Ben had blown that flame out. "What do you mean, stay?" he'd shouted. He'd done everything he could to argue his way out of there. He said it was dangerous for her. He said he could do more in the field. He called it being "sidetracked." Whatever he called it, it all boiled down to the same thing; he wanted out.

She understood. She could even live with it. It must have been a nesting thing, wanting a man around, wanting his arms around her. Loneliness and hormones packed a powerful kick. Wanting him there was an aberration, just like the kiss they'd shared had been. She just wished he wouldn't keep rubbing it in.

"I wouldn't have even come here if I hadn't needed help."

"I know that."

"It could have put you in danger. You could be in danger still."

She doubted his idea of danger and hers meshed. Living under the same roof with Ben put her emotions on a windy cliff. Thank God she hadn't thrown her arms around his neck earlier; she'd never have lived it down. Now she could pretend an indifference she didn't feel.

"I wouldn't have left without thanking you."

"No thanks necessary." She fluffed a pillow—with both fists.

"I wanted to spare you, in case anyone came around asking questions. I know I did a lot of lying."

That wasn't all he'd done. Somewhere along the line he'd begun to matter to her, to matter so much she wanted to spit nails, cry sizzling tears, and throw things, the more breakable the better.

"Now that you're part of this, I can tell you whatever you want to know."

So why did you kiss me like that last night? She swung her hands wide, her voice overly bright. "You're my guest; that's all I need to know. Watch smugglers come and go to your heart's content." She folded the coverlet to a knife's edge.

Ben shifted weight onto his injured leg. He grunted as if he deserved the pain. The side of his fist butted against the window frame. "I know you don't want me here."

"Did I say that?"

"You haven't said anything else."

"You made it clear you didn't like Stonesmith's idea any more than I did."

"I could do more in the field, see more. What

good is it going to do, me sitting here with a telescope? I feel like Jimmy Stewart in *Rear Window*."

"If you see anyone digging graves in the garden, let me know. I need those tomatoes for salads." She sashayed around the head of the angled bed to the telescope's tripod. "Laser sights, computerized direction finder. It looks very complicated. How did he know you'd need it?"

Pinned by her gaze, he gave her the truth. "I called him."

"When?"

"Last night after you went to bed."

That hurt too. "I called when I said I did."

"I believed you. I also knew you'd get the runaround; that number never goes through. It's an alert, a trace. I called them later to fill them in on the details."

"Like the background on the house? My trying to give up cigarettes? My brother?" That last word brought steel to her spine.

"They had to check you out."

"To see if I could be trusted."

"It's a hazard of the trade."

"You couldn't have vouched for me?" She brushed a spiky bang from her forehead. Swiping the spare towels from the bed, she headed for the door.

He stared at her retreating shoulders. "After last night I barely trusted myself to stay on the couch, much less give an objective report about you."

She looked at the varnished floorboards.

"What was I supposed to tell them, that she melts faster than snow when you kiss the side of her neck? That her skin glows like warm embers when you touch her breasts?"

Her lower lip trembled.

"You don't know how close I came to climbing those stairs last night."

"You'd have never made it."

"We almost did."

He watched the confusion in her eyes war with the flicker of remembered desire and the pain of his betrayal. They'd treated her like the enemy. He didn't blame her for being angry. It was only right she take it out on him. He knew better than Stonesmith how giving she was, how vulnerable. He should have defended her then. He had to keep his hands off her now; it was the only way they'd survive.

He straightened, his leg reminding him how long he'd been standing. "I've got to stay. For however long I'm here, we need to get along."

She picked up her cue. Blinking rapidly, she forced a smile. "I'm an expert at coddling guests. Especially the grumbling ones who don't think they need a vacation."

"This is purely a working vacation."

"See?"

"I'll need a wake-up call at four."

"A.M.? Guess again."

"P.M. I'll stay up all night then sleep through the days. I don't think they're brazen enough to unload in broad daylight."

"Then you're going to bed?"

"I was going to try." He waited, wondering if the words whirled through her mind the way they did through his, unsaid, unsayable.

She opened the door. "It's nearly noon. I'll knock at four."

"What time do you go to bed?"

"Around eleven."

"Will you stop in before then?"

"Why?"

He looked at her as if the answer were perfectly obvious. "So I can say good night."

Bridget found herself doing it again, placing her palm to her chest and breathing deep. Her hands shook; fine, she could blame that on nicotine. It was the deeper quiver, the fine tremble in her limbs each time she thought of him upstairs that gave her pause. The only way this arrangement would work was if she kept it strictly impersonal.

"Shouldn't be hard." It had been three days and nights since he'd moved into her room, and already he was giving orders. "The man has a natural talent for leadership."

Making the soup she planned to have for dinner and to feed him for breakfast, she tossed another plate of carrots into the soup pot and waited for it to boil again. " 'Bring me this. Bring me that.' Who does he think he is?"

He'd just finished scolding her for leaving her light on too late the night before. Whose fault was it if she couldn't sleep? Stephen King's *Insomnia* had sat on her lap unread while she'd stared at her reflection in the window. She was in a strange room in a strange bed and the layout bugged her no end. By the time she'd dragged the bed to a better vantage point and rearranged the chairs, he'd been knocking on the wall. Who knew logs carried sound so well?

She'd marched over to his room, knocked once, and gone in. "Please don't dictate when I can and can't work. I've taken on this huge project, solo, and I'm losing I don't know how many hours catering to you."

He'd sat with his back to her in the center of the tower, one hand resting on the telescope. Norman Bates's mother couldn't have sat stiller. "Just remember to turn off the light. Things should look as normal as possible."

She'd stormed back to her room and slammed the door, turning off the lamp with a vicious flick of her wrist. Turning off her emotions was considerably harder. She was furious with him. With herself. She felt hurt, ignored, lonely, and she hated every minute of it. His feelings for her had cooled so quickly, she wondered if she'd imagined them. She was getting obsessive, emotional, touchy. "If I didn't know better, I'd blame it on PMS."

She dashed a handful of pepper into the soup and patted her flat stomach. She was cooking for two now, just not the two she'd expected. She looked at the bright side. A woman couldn't fall in love with a dream when reality moved in. In a month they'd be sick of each other. In two she'd be the one eager to see him leave.

It would be so easy if she liked him a tad less. "I'm working on it."

She rolled her head from one side to the other. Every muscle ached. She glanced at the phone and thought of checking up on Richie. It was five o'clock. Time to take Ben the first meal of his day and the last of hers.

❖————————————❖

Ben glared at the horizon line, jarred awake by something. He grasped the telescope, peering at the charcoal clouds hanging heavy over the lake's obsidian surface. No movement, no lights, no ships. He pressed a button on his watch, cupping it out of habit. The glowing numbers told him he'd been asleep less than fifteen minutes. He sighed with relief and sat back. Sleeping on the job; he'd have to note it in his log. What if he'd missed something important?

A keening sound whistled through the chimney, bringing with it the tangy scent of charred pine. A damp draft slithered through the flue. Someone sniffed.

Ben turned his head. In the darkness he barely made out her profile on the window seat. Behind her, stars pinpricked a patch of clear sky. It was a quarter after two in the morning. "Bridget?"

After a long moment she cleared her throat. "Am I bothering you? You were concentrating."

"I was asleep."

"Did I wake you?"

"If you did, I'm glad."

She said nothing. They sat for minutes in tense silence. He wanted to ask what she was doing there. He feared he'd chase her away.

She sniffed and stood, pulling a shawl around her shoulders. "I don't want to interfere with your work."

His hand shot out. She'd interfered with everything else, his equilibrium, his sense of priorities. Smugglers were out there somewhere. But she was here. "What is it?"

Her arms clutched across her chest. He eased his thumb into her palm, rubbing, cajoling. He studied the roundness of her cheek, the delicate profile. It soothed the urgency he'd felt when he thought he was about to lose her. "What is it?"

"Just wanted some company," she whispered. "I should let you work."

"Nothing out there now. Anyway, I could use the company."

She nudged a throw pillow aside and took a place on the window seat. Ben shoved his chair closer, a clumsy maneuver considering what little help he got from his bad leg. After five days the wound was more a nuisance than a handicap. After sitting all evening, his thigh was stiff and uncooperative. "Hope that didn't scratch your floor."

Her sniff served as a laugh.

It seemed imperative that he hold on to her. Their joined hands rested on the arm of his chair. Her shawl was a scratchy-soft mohair. It glimmered with glints of metallic thread, as silvery as the tear streaks on her cheeks. "What's wrong?"

"Nothing."

He tugged on her hand, cursing himself for being so bad at this. If he'd had any idea how to treat a crying woman, he might still be married. "What is it?"

She shrugged. The waves hushed onto the beach below them. "I lost the baby."

NINE

He gritted his teeth, unsure what to say. There were no words for this.

She wiped her cheek with the back of her hand. "I shouldn't say that. I probably never had it."

"You're not pregnant then?"

"The insemination must not have worked." She sighed. "Can't lose what you never had."

Ben resisted the impulse to grip her hand until it hurt. She was trying to make the best of the situation. He did what little he could. "You wanted that baby."

"How would you know?"

"The way your eyes lit up when you talked about it."

She gave him a teasing smile. "You yelled at me when I talked about it."

He squeezed her hand, wishing every now and then someone would come along and give him the swift kick in the pants he deserved. "So I'm an idiot. It sounded nuts and clinical and scientific when it should be romantic and committed and—hell. You wanted it, that's what matters."

"Very much." Her lips barely moved.

"Who am I to say what's right and wrong, especially when it comes to stuff like this? I'm no expert."

"But you have one." Her eyes raised to his, her wet lashes like spiky stars. "You have a baby."

"She's not a baby anymore. She's started school." He waited for her to bring him up short for neglecting his own child when she was trying so hard to have one. They sat in silence instead. Another tear slid down her cheek.

He wrestled with the temptation to wipe the tear away with his thumb. He combed her hair behind her ear first, the better to see her in the faint light of a waning moon. "I am sorry."

Another shrug. Another shudder that sounded like a stifled sob. "It's not your fault."

"The stress of all this could have—"

"No." Her urgency immediately subsided. She clasped his hand in both of hers and removed it to the safety of her lap, patting it gently. "How many people get pregnant on the first try? I knew it might not happen. I kept reminding myself— Silly of me to get my hopes up, that's all." She sniffed again, then wiped her face with a corner of the shawl. She pointed toward the window. "Where do you expect to spot your smugglers?"

He let her change the subject. If she wanted to talk shop, he'd talk shop. Whatever Bridget wanted suddenly mattered more than anything. "Initially I was tracking their movements inland, figuring where they unloaded and where they stored their stuff. From here I'm charting what boats come and go and when. I'll

make a tally over a couple of months, see what corre-
lates with boats leaving Canadian marinas. We want to
build an airtight case on both sides of the lake, pinpoint the whole organization from top to bottom."

She smiled faintly, her fingers unconsciously twining with his. "Why do I get the feeling you're making
the best of this?"

He grimaced. "Because I like to be on the ground,
in the middle of the action. I like to see who I'm putting away. What?"

"You sound different when you talk that way.
Tough. Determined."

"What do I usually sound like?"

"Grumpy. Bossy. Frustrated."

He grunted, stung by her good-natured jabs. "I
don't mean to take it out on you."

"I'm getting used to it." Her laugh subsided into a
sigh. "I know you don't want to be here, Ben."

"Says who?"

"Said you to Stonesmith."

"I didn't see what purpose it would serve. I
thought for sure you'd scream bloody murder about it.
Hell, I landed on your doorstep and I've been nothing
but a lying pack of trouble since."

"You keep apologizing for that."

"I'll lie to dealers and crooks anytime. Not many
women appreciate a man whose specialty is playing
both sides."

Self-conscious, she stared out over the lake. Good
thing someone was watching for activity; he couldn't
tear his gaze from her face.

"You don't give yourself enough credit," she said
quietly. "You're a very giving man."

Only around her. He took her hand in his again.

"Hey, don't you comfort me. That's supposed to be my job."

She wiped her face. "This isn't really your problem."

"It is now."

"I should have waited until I knew it was real."

Straining to make out her eyes in the darkness, he struggled to find the right words.. "What happens now? Do you want me to take you to a doctor?"

"It's just a period. If it was a miscarriage, I think it'd hurt more."

He saw plenty of hurt.

"I'll have to go back to the clinic and try again next month." Her resolve faltered with her voice. "Or maybe the month after. I might need a little time to work up to it again. You picture them, you know? Who they'll turn out to be and how much you'll love them." Her voice caught.

He wished he could move closer and knew his leg wouldn't cooperate. It'd be a clumsy series of maneuvers, as unnatural as—as getting pregnant via syringe. Distance be damned. He bent his bad knee and lurched out of the chair. He did one thing right; he got her to scoot over so he could put his good thigh alongside hers. He wrapped his arm around her shoulders.

It had been a week since he'd held her in front of the fireplace. In that short time he'd forgotten how well she fit, how her hair cushioned his chin when he rested it on the crown of her head. He kissed it, then urged her cheek to his chest. "It'll be okay."

He felt the frail strength that held her together. "Thank you for your concern. It's very sweet of you."

He glared at the lake. They didn't need to play it

formal, not the way they did in the daytime, not this late at night. He scanned the horizon one more time, satisfied nothing was moving. Waves came and went; stars flickered.

He kissed her hair again, tenderly, selfishly. He memorized the way her body heat spread through his chest. He'd removed the bandage around his ribs that afternoon when he'd showered. His chest hair caught and crinkled against the slippery fabric of her satin wrap. He wondered how it would feel against her skin. He remembered her breast in his hand, the hot feel of her flesh in front of the fireplace.

A sigh escaped him. He was a jerk. He shouldn't even be thinking these things, much less letting his body react. She'd come to him for comfort. He did his clumsy best. "Are you going to be okay?"

She nodded, her face warm against his skin, her hand a small fist above his right nipple.

"Are you sure?"

She nodded again.

He rubbed her back, long strokes and circular ones. He traced where her waist narrowed and let his hands rove over the flare of her hips. "I never had any sisters, you know."

She sniffed. "I didn't know that."

"The only woman I ever lived with was Carla. However, as I recall, at this time of the month a back rub feels good."

Her laugh had a hitch, but at least it was a laugh. "You learned that lesson well. It feels great."

"Then I won't stop." He kneaded her, smiling grimly at the pun. He didn't want to think how much he needed her or how long it was since he'd held a woman. Vaguely wondering what the difference was between a stroke and a caress, he discovered he didn't care. He'd touch her all night if she let him.

He spanned her back with both hands, eventually bringing the massage to her shoulders, her arms, and down to her wrists.

"Those aren't sore," she murmured.

"No? What about here?" He slid his palms up her shoulders, working the tension gathered at the base of her neck.

She moaned and let her head fall back. "How did you guess?"

"Just luck." And experience. From the first time she'd bandaged him, he'd had his own taste of tension. But his was of a slightly different kind. It started in his shoulders but quickly, inexorably, moved downward. He imagined the kind of massage necessary to cure that ache. It would stretch body to body, limb to limb.

He deliberately broke the rhythm, returning to long strokes up and down her back.

She folded against him, resting her face on his shoulder. Her breasts skimmed his chest through her nightgown. "I shouldn't be such a baby about this."

She was all woman. He meant to tell her.

"I should have known it might not work out."

"Nobody knows how things will work out." A man could commit himself, though, vow to make it work. Even then, a man could fail no matter how hard he tried. At that point it was better to give up. Why drag anyone else through the special hell known as a crumbling marriage?

Not that life with Carla had been anything like this. He'd never associated marriage with this sense of peace and limitless desire. It went beyond physical

Save 85% Off The Cover Price on 4 *Loveswept*® Romances

need. It was who she was, how he felt with her, how necessary.

"What was it like when you had your baby?"

He laughed quietly. "You'd have to ask Carla. It didn't look easy."

She thumped his chest. "I meant to you."

"Me? You asked that before."

"Tell me again. The birth part."

He took a minute to gather the memories. "I remember a lot of yelling, a lot of breathing, a lot of blood. There were words I didn't even know my wife knew, most of them directed at me for getting her pregnant."

Bridget chuckled.

Ben found himself smiling. "Then there was this wrinkled blue baby and nurses in green masks telling me that's what she was supposed to look like. Then they let me hold her, this little baby, this little life, no bigger than my two hands put together. I'd never wanted to protect anything so much in my life." Until now. The thought vibrated through him like a small but familiar earthquake. She'd become more important to him every day, starting that first night when she'd let him in, so brave with that fireplace poker in her hand, that dusty gun.

Bridget put her arms around his waist. It seemed so natural. He combed her hair off her damp cheek, rocking her gently. "That's the story of my short-lived parenthood. She was two years old when her mother and I split up. Carla's choice."

She looked up at him.

"Mine too. If you can't do something right, don't do it at all. That's my motto."

Her lips parted as if she wanted to argue. "You

should take what life offers, no matter what the circumstances."

Should he? He bent his head, brushing his lips over hers.

For a second he thought she'd push him away. Her hands splayed on his chest. His heart contracted. He tried to think of the last time a woman had touched him. He remembered as far back as Bridget nursing him, bathing his wounds.

But that had been in sickness. This was in health. He moved her hand to his nipple, feeling her fingers curl in the crinkled hair. Everything she did set him on fire. Her kiss, a simple thank you made his heart thump. She took his face in her hands and tilted it downward, the better to plant a soft kiss on his temple.

"You're very understanding," she said. "Thank you."

It was only the beginning. He thanked her.

"For what?"

He nodded at her hands on him.

She shyly framed his face, combing her fingers through his hair, her nails doing sinful things to his scalp. When her fingertips skimmed his ear he sucked in a breath.

"You saved my life," he said. He was the one who owed *her*.

"You saved mine," she replied. "Or tried to. Remember the popcorn?"

"I made a fool of myself."

"You're a better man than you know. Hasn't anyone told you that?"

Not in so many words. She managed to convey it with one touch. Fire flared in him, a pounding pulse.

She found his mouth again. Her tongue grazed his. The very hint of her hunger ignited him. He pulled back, wanting to savor it, devour it. That kind of hunger might be fine if they were both ready. She'd come to him in tears. He'd be a heel to rush her. "Are you sure you're all right?"

She blinked, her eyes dewy, her lips moist. "I'm fine."

She wasn't. She seemed mesmerized, intent on touching him, exploring every inch. She ran her hands through his hair again, strands filtering through her fingers.

"Bridget."

His raspy warning made her smile, a wonder-filled, moonstruck smile he'd remember to the last night of his life. Her fingers slid the length of his throat. She gloried in the way he swallowed the lump in it. She seemed to discover for the first time that he was naked from the waist up. "Aren't you chilly?"

"Do I feel chilly?"

She shyly played both hands across his upper chest. The fire was unmistakable. It radiated off his skin. She gingerly dropped her hands to his ribs. "Does it still hurt?" she asked.

Honey, it's going to break in two and fall off if you don't stop that. She'd meant his ribs. "Only hurts when I breathe hard. You could kiss it and make it better."

Dared, tempted, she bent her head. She swept a handful of hair over the nape of her neck, the better to skim her lips across his bruised side. "Better?"

"Lower."

It was shadowy down there. Her fingers blindly explored the next rib. She kissed its length from his side to his abdomen. Then she moved down to the next. "Lower?" she asked.

She caught on fast.

Ben gripped her arms and lifted her to him, angling her so the moonlight washed her face in pale light. He knew what he intended to say. Before he said it, he wanted her to know he meant it.

That's why he kissed her, her face, her throat, the side of her neck under a handful of hair. She gasped, and he did it all again, harder this time. He'd never expected her to be shy; his Bridget was too full of life, too open to its twists and turns, too honest. When he rasped an unshaven cheek against her throat, she moaned for more. He tugged her robe open, smearing sandpaper kisses over the mound of her left breast.

He wanted to give her everything he could, to lay her beneath him and fit his body to hers, in hers. He wanted her hands on him and her legs around him. He wanted her moaning his name when he thrust into her. When she shuddered deep inside he wanted to touch the source of that quiver.

More than any of it, he wanted her to know what was happening was more than sex. "I meant it," he said, his voice unnaturally harsh. "What I said the other night, about giving you a baby."

Her heavy-lidded eyes widened. Her voice was a puff of air. "What?"

"If that's what you want, Bridget. Let me give it to you."

She shook her head, backing away.

He pulled her to him, their bodies aligned from the waist up. "I wasn't much as a husband. I never had much chance to be a father. But I could do this. For you. You need a man, not an experiment. Someone

you know, with a face, a past. You could look at your
child and know where he came from." And who he
came from.

"Why?"

Because she needed it, Ben thought. Because it was
the closest he could ever come to her. Because seeing
her cry tore a path through him more jagged than any
bullet. It opened something in him; a need to be
needed, to be useful. When he left—and he knew he'd
have to sooner or later—he wanted to leave part of
himself with her. It was a fair exchange; he'd carry
memories of her as long as he lived. "Let me do this."

She blinked again, this time in sheer consternation. She shook her head, agitation rising. "You
can't."

"I'm not that wounded."

"I mean, it wouldn't do any good. Not now. Not
this time of the month."

"A week from now, two weeks. Whatever's best
for you. I'll still be here."

She stood, fiddling with the tie around her waist,
running both hands through her hair as if trying to
hold her head on her shoulders. "I don't know
whether to laugh or run and lock myself in my room."

"You want this."

"A baby, yes, but this—" She waved a limp wrist at
him, shooing him like a fly. "This isn't exactly something you make an appointment for! Two weeks from
today we'll meet in my bedroom?"

"Any day, any time. I don't think we'd have a
problem."

She planted her feet as he struggled to his. "That's
not what I meant. This is not the time to discuss this."

She was absolutely right. "I rushed you. I didn't mean to. You don't have to do anything right now."

"I don't have to do anything ever," she retorted in alarm.

"Bridget, I—" He scraped a hand through his hair. "God, I'm screwing this up."

"I'm sorry I interrupted you, your work," she rattled on, backing for the door. "I don't know why I came. I didn't mean for you to misunderstand, I just needed somebody—"

And he'd turned it into something else.

"I'm sorry, Ben."

She was sorry? He was beating himself to a pulp for mishandling things. "Bridget, I just wanted to help, to repay you."

"Oh, that does it." She swung open the door, her robe flying as she whirled to a halt. "You don't owe me anything. Let's just forget this ever happened."

"Bridget!"

The door's slam echoed down the hall.

Bridget shoved off from her bedroom door, turned on the small lamp on the end table, and stormed to her bed. She lasted five seconds under the covers before she kicked them off and resumed pacing. How could he? How could she? Of course he'd misinterpreted her coming to his room. The tears were honest, the grief sincere. But the kisses had been just as real. She'd led him on, touching him, loving every minute of it.

She bowed her head and held it in both hands. She felt sick, achy, empty. She felt humiliated, and there was only one person to blame.

He knocked on her door.

"I know what you're going to say," she called. " 'Turn out the light.' " She strode to the table and switched it off. "Done. Good night."

He opened her door.

"Ben—"

The light flicked on, a warm golden glow that emphasized the shirt he'd thrown on but hadn't buttoned. The burnished tones of his olive skin shone amid patches of hair she'd just finished kissing. She forced her gaze to his face. His black hair had never looked blacker, his features bleaker.

"That's not what I'm here for," he said.

A faint tremble coursed through her. "Get out." She barely breathed the words.

"Get in bed."

She took one step back. Another.

He took her arm and steered her to the bed. "Sit down."

Speechless, she complied. "I didn't invite you in here. This is my room."

"Next door is your room and I took it." He thumped the pillows against the headboard and sat down, lifting his bad leg onto the bed. "Come here."

She didn't move.

"It's time I gave you some TLC." He reached for her waist, turned her, and pulled her behind into the vee of his spread legs. Folding one arm over her waist, he combed her hair off her forehead with his free hand. "I'm sorry," he whispered, his breath warm on her cheek. "I said all the wrong things at the wrong time and took this way past what you wanted."

She shook her head. He hadn't done it all. She'd been guilty too.

He wouldn't hear of it. "I should've done this from the start."

"Done what?"

"Held you." His chest supported her back. He urged her head back against his shoulder, rocking her gently.

She shifted her hips to fit better between his thighs. Gradually she relaxed into him. From over her shoulder, his cheek pressed to hers.

"It'll be okay," he whispered.

It was better than okay. And much worse. The anger had kept the hurt at bay. So had the shock of his offer. For a fragment of a moment she'd forgotten about the baby she'd lost, forgotten how it hurt to lose a dream. It would hurt even more if she let this become one, if she let herself love someone who wouldn't and couldn't stay.

Silently, she let the tears come. She folded her arms over his. "I didn't mean for that to happen."

"Neither did I. Not so quick."

"Could you just hold me awhile?"

"Baby, I could do this all night."

She curled her knees up, letting him cradle her. Emotionally spent, she drifted into a numb sleep.

Ben rocked her until the sun came up. He asked himself a hundred times what he was letting himself in for. But the woman in his arms held the answers. Hold her all night? He could hold her for the rest of his life.

TEN

Her mind mellow as mist, her body as warm as slept-in sheets, Bridget opened her eyes and a glinting slice of lake swam into view. A beautiful brisk northern morning. Tucked in a fetal position, she searched her mind for her morning plans, which designs she'd work on today, which rooms. This early, her thoughts were never well ordered. She wasn't surprised when Ben invaded them, his body, his scent, how good he'd tasted, how he'd feel beside her in the morning.

She stretched her arms over her head and rolled onto her back. Before she got there, her rear end bumped a solid object.

"Morning."

She froze. Craning her neck, she scanned the length of him. He half sat, half leaned against the headboard, his legs extended in front of him. She'd curled into a ball beside him.

His good leg was bent to support her back. She'd snuggled into that support. Even in her sleep she'd longed to be closer to him. Her skin still held the imprint of his hand resting on her back. "I fell asleep," she said stupidly.

He grinned and bent to kiss her. The heavy black wings of his hair fell forward, casting his eyes in gray morning shadow, tantalizingly soft compared with the previous night's powerful darkness.

She slanted a guilty look his way, desperate to remember the previous night. Relaxed, happy, sexy as all get out, he grinned right back.

She gulped. "What time is it?"

"Time for me to call it a night."

Had she worn him out that badly? He still had his slacks on, but his chest was bare beneath his open shirt. Her palms tingled as she recalled the feel of that chest. Her lips had planted kisses all down his torso.

He nuzzled her nose. "You look groggy."

"I'm practically in a stupor."

He was little help. That too-early grin irritated her caffeine-deprived nervous system no end. "To answer your question," he rasped out, "it's seven A.M. My bedtime and your wake-up call." He slung an arm around her shoulders as she sat up.

Heat flushed her cheeks at the familiar protective way he held her. She loved it. She shouldn't. She gave him an imploring look. "About last night—"

"The offer's still open."

The offer. Her heart thudded to a stop. She threw back the afghan he'd thrown over her, rapidly tugging her nightgown down where it had ridden up. "I should get you your breakfast. Dinner. Whatever you call it."

"Know what I really want?"

"A cigarette?" she muttered. "I'd kill for one right now."

"How about a walk?"

"A walk?"

"It's healthier. Besides, we could both use the exercise."

As long as it wasn't the horizontal kind.

He angled his leg off the bed, his body stiff after sitting so long.

"Are you sure you're up for it?"

He cocked a brow her way. "The offer or the walk?"

She scowled and raced for her dresser. "If your leg is better, sure, let's get some fresh air. That's a great idea. You must be feeling awfully cooped up."

"I'm feeling something," he murmured.

She didn't dare turn around. Grabbing her baggy jeans and the bulkiest sweater she owned, she decided layers were the key. It was a brisk morning—if her taut nipples were any indication. She held the clothes to her chest. "Want me to get you a heavier shirt?"

"I can manage. Meet you in the hall in ten minutes."

She released a pent-up breath when he limped out the door. The frantic activity had cleared her mind. She'd done nothing to be ashamed of. Not that loving him would be shameful, just risky to her equilibrium and emotional well-being. Not to mention her entire self-concept as a woman. She believed in seizing life, but that didn't mean plunging headlong into relationships that could never work.

A small voice whispered in her head. Who was she to say how life was supposed to work? Life worked however it wanted. The important thing was to live it as it came. And not get burned in the process.

His offer was beyond considering. Their caresses

of the night before had been more wonderful than she cared to remember. But that was then. By the light of day she saw more clearly. They'd be friends. They'd be roommates in a twenty-eight-room house. And from now on she'd keep her hands to herself.

She'd gone to him in tears because she'd needed to be near him. He'd gotten the chivalrous, outlandish idea that he was the man to solve her problems, that somehow this was his responsibility. She could handle her life herself. *And* her libido.

Bridget scampered over an exposed hump of granite, inhaling a rich mix of dry grasses and moss along the Lake Superior shore. The sunlight falling across the clearing felt sinfully sensual after the cool shadows of the woods. Ben limped into the opening, his cane ticking against the rock ledge.

"Keeping up?" she asked.

He grunted. The effort of the last few feet tightened the corners of his mouth.

"How's the leg?"

"Great."

"Like an obstacle course is great? Like basic training is great?"

"Like watching your pert behind when you climb these rocks."

"Pert?" Her laughter bubbled over. "I thought you'd appreciate the view."

He leered at her.

She clamped her hands on his arms and physically turned him. "That one. From Keeweenaw Point and Manitou Island to"—another half turn—"Bête Grise lighthouse. See it? Yellow with blue trim."

"I see it," he said, his gaze resting on her brown eyes.

She didn't dare ask what he saw when he looked at her. His mouth thinned in a determined line.

"Want to head back to the house yet?" she asked.

"Do you?" It sounded like a sultry invitation. "We haven't eaten that breakfast you made."

She swayed the picnic basket at her side. "I say we spread the tablecloth right here. There's sun, a breeze, the lake, and the view. You can spy all you want." And she could busy herself laying out plastic dishes and paper plates. "Croissants, bagels, jam, cream cheese, fruit, juices in boxes."

"I'll have one of each. I'm famished."

She knelt, arranging everything just so as Ben struggled to sit. She knew he wouldn't appreciate too much help. "You're staring."

"I think the walk did you as much good as it's doing me."

It did wonders for her achiness. It hadn't done a thing for the lingering sense of anticipation she was feeling. He'd very seriously offered to get her pregnant. She couldn't let him know how the idea nagged at her. Every time she dismissed it out of hand, it slunk back into her mind. She studied him surreptitiously, picturing a baby with blue eyes and unruly, ruler-straight black hair.

They ate. The bluff was twenty feet above a narrow strip of beach. Ben stretched out, one elbow supporting him. He glanced over the edge. "There's no sand down there."

Bridget craned her neck. Water washed over flat slabs of ocher-colored stone striped with white clay.

Light sliced through the waves, fluttering over the stones in undulating lines. "Beautiful, isn't it?"

"No diving here."

"Not much boating either." She indicated the granite ledges jutting from the water a hundred feet from shore, stony sentinels reddish brown with iron.

She pointed with her bagel. "One of my first projects was checking out the frontage. A mile that way there's nothing but sand. Another mile and there's black sand. If smugglers are putting in somewhere nearby, it would have to be there. Less risky."

"If they worried about risk, they wouldn't take on Lake Superior in anything less than an ore boat. Amazing what people will do to make money the hard way. How about heading that way after breakfast?"

She paused, the bagel halfway to her lips. She'd thought they'd eat, then limp back home. She hadn't envisioned spending the day with him.

He noticed her surprise. "If they've been here, they may have left footprints, some sign of activity."

"An arrow in the sand saying, 'Smugglers Hideout: This Way'?"

He ignored her lighthearted sarcasm. "Criminals have been known to do dumber things. Like the guy who robbed a bank wearing a football jersey with his name embroidered on the back. Anyway, they don't know we're here or that we're looking for them."

"They shot at you."

"I thought of that. Stonesmith said he got an article in the *Mining Gazette* saying a hunter had been found dead in the woods. If they think the heat's off, they might get sloppy." He dragged a knifeful of jam over a bagel. "Pick me up a copy when you're in town next time, okay?"

"You want a copy of your death notice?"

"Probably the only one I'll be around to read."

She set her breakfast down, her appetite fading. "I don't know why you do it."

"I believe in law and order."

"So do I. That doesn't mean risking your life for it."

"What else would I risk it for?"

Her eyes met his and held. She could think of a hundred things. She looked out at the lake. "This has to be one of the most beautiful spots on earth."

His gaze rested on her. "Yes, it is."

"Don't toy with me, Renfield. The nicotine withdrawal has eased, but the temper's intact."

He chuckled, twisting carefully to look out over the water. "This whole coast is perfect for secluded landings."

Seclusion was good for other things, Bridget thought. There they sat, pretending they were having a civilized brunch while she tried to chase away thoughts of two people chaperoned by nothing but wildflowers, wildlife, and the occasional wheeling seagull. She needn't have worried. Studying the chiseled line of his jaw, the clear-cut determination in his eyes, she realized he was caught up in his work.

"They could use the lighthouse as a landmark," he mused. "Easy to steer by that. The lodge wouldn't be bad either. Those white logs stand out."

"Still, at night I'd have to put a light in the window."

That light had drawn him, saved him. She drew him now. Ben rolled onto his side, tired with effort instead of pain. He'd been calling in his observations every day, relaying the facts. Thinking aloud, letting someone in on his thought processes was unheard of. He marveled at how natural sharing felt with her. "Nix the light idea. We don't want to attract them, just spy on them."

"We?"

"Unless you're signaling someone," he teased dryly.

"No thanks. No drugs to sell today."

Guilt gave him a twinge of pain. "Stonesmith never meant you were in on this."

"I thought I was about to be fingerprinted."

"Strictly speaking, it's not the most legal thing in the world, mailing out drugs like catalog orders."

"You needed them."

"Dammit, Bridget, you send it through the mail, it's a federal offense."

"And who are you, Dudley Doright? You were in pain, if you recall. You could hardly sleep."

What were they arguing about? He blamed it on lack of sleep. There were days he lay awake listening for her in the hall, the sound of her humming, the scrape of a ladder being moved. He felt worse than useless. His growing energy had transformed itself into a restlessness he had no way to expend. He'd meant for their walk to work it off. And it had, temporarily.

"Not that you're sleeping much anyway," she muttered.

How did she know? "How do you mean?"

She cleaned a jar rim with her thumb, licking off the sticky reddish jam. It almost matched the color of her lips. "I mean you're up all night watching for boats."

"I've seen a few."

"You've spotted them?" She leaned forward excitedly.

"More than once. The hard part is pinpointing where they're putting in. We want to catch them at their base. That way we might snag some of their local contacts."

"You think someone around here is involved?"

"Could be. Could even be local law enforcement. The trick is snagging everyone at once. Arrest them on land, and you lose the shippers. Arrest them at sea—"

"And you've got a fabulous pirate movie. Prepare to be boarded, ye maties!" Her salty cackle echoed in the surrounding trees. Her mischievous grin was even more captivating. "Richie and I had a pool when we were kids. One summer we built an entire regatta of model ships."

"Sounds like a neat childhood."

"Portable pool, suburban backyard, nothing special. I built the ship models, and he sewed the pirates' costumes. Don't laugh."

He swallowed a smile.

"Oh, all right, laugh. My architectural tendencies were evident even then, as was Richie's artistic side. He always said he was a walking cliché. Says," she corrected.

Ben sat up. He reached across the cloth to hold her hand. "How sick is he?"

"A little worse. It comes and goes. I talked to him last night, before—before I came to see you. I didn't mean to disturb you."

The only thing that disturbed him was her trying to handle this alone. "You didn't tell him about my staying, did you?"

"I've been ordered not to."

"That doesn't exactly answer the question."

"He's my brother."

"Meaning you told him?"

Affronted, she sat back on her heels. "You sound as if you don't trust me."

She still hadn't answered. "You have this way of deciding for yourself what's right and what's wrong."

"If I don't decide, who will?"

"The law, for one."

"Is this about those pills again? Richie's known too many people in pain to sit by and do nothing."

"That doesn't make it legal."

She spat out an expletive that pinned his ears back. "Legal schmegal. What matters is what works."

"Situational ethics. Choosing what's right from moment to moment and person to person."

"Ah, now I'm getting a lecture from Mr. I-Can't-Tell-a-Lie?"

He sighed, momentarily defeated by her ability to deflect a perfectly good argument with a teasing twinkle of her eye. "Every blessed one of them failed around you. You saw through me from the start."

She shrugged, reaching naturally, comfortably, for his hand.

"I could have been some escaped criminal."

She wasn't the least intimidated. "You? Never. There was something about you. Something noble, reassuring, trustworthy."

He snorted. "I don't look like John Wayne, and I only walk this way because of a bullet."

"You're about as conservative as him."

"And what's wrong with that? Break the rules, you get put away. That's all there is to it."

"Very black-and-white."

"I believe in knowing right from wrong."

"And lying to people when it suits you. And black-mailing people into letting you stay."

"That wasn't me."

She let his hand slip from hers as she tidied up the picnic basket. "You would have gone if you could."

"I didn't want you involved; I wouldn't risk that."

"Except for Mr. Stonesmith, no one's come snooping."

"They still could."

"If they do, I'll happily lie through my teeth and say the house is private and off-limits."

"Which brings me back to my original question."

"Which was?"

"Did you tell Richie I was staying?"

"No. You don't believe me?"

"You wouldn't have given me all this runaround if it was no."

"I didn't tell him. Not because you or Stonesmith said I couldn't, but because I don't want him worrying. He's got enough on his mind."

Ben paused before treading on sensitive territory. "Did you tell him about the baby?"

She stared out at the water. Drawing up one knee, she balanced her elbow on it and lost her fingers in the tangles of her hair. "Not yet. He's been as excited about it as me. He wanted me to have a boy so I'd name it after him. It doesn't take Freud to figure out why. He wants someone to live on after him. So do I." She diverted an ant from her sandal, sweeping it off the cloth.

"Is that the main reason you wanted a child?"

"There are lots of reasons. When we first learned

Richie was sick, I found myself thinking, "What would *I* do if I learned I had a limited time to live? What would I wish I'd done?' Having a baby was top of the list."

She tilted her head, resting her chin on her hand. Her chestnut hair caught the sun's rays. Her big brown eyes studied him. "What I don't understand is why you risk *your* life."

"Mine?" He shrugged that off as if it were nothing. "Comes with the territory."

"Don't get glib, Mr. Wayne."

He thought it through. "As long as there are people willing to kill for what they want, somebody's got to be willing to stand in their way."

That was the prime reason he'd stayed. Although, as she said, there were a lot of reasons. He knew he might be endangering her by staying in her house. It'd be worse if he left her alone. Who would stop the smugglers if they spotted the lodge and decided to use it as their port of call? It would be criminally easy. Once in, they could get her out of the way or keep her around for amusement. The thought turned his stomach.

"So you're willing to risk your life for what you believe," she said.

"It's not that melodramatic. I only risk my life on Tuesdays and Thursdays. The rest is paperwork."

Stretching out, she pressed her back into the sun-warm rock. She bent her forearm over her eyes to shield them from the sun. "What's it really like?"

"Nothing glamorous. I go from place to place. Sometimes I have to fit in. Other times I watch from a distance. Someday I'll tell you about the motorcycle-gang initiation."

"Someday." She smiled.

They both knew that day might never come. He had an urge to tell her more, to share what he could while he could. He'd been wrong to make it sound easy, as if after this job, he'd merely move on to the next. Leaving her behind wouldn't be easy.

"So where do you live?" she asked out of the blue.

"An apartment in the Atlanta area."

"Centrally located."

"That's the idea."

She squinted at a cloud. "So why do I picture empty walls, a refrigerator with three outdated items on its otherwise empty shelves, and a pile of bills lying on the floor just inside the mail slot?"

"I'm sure you'd do wonders with it."

"That's *my* job. Where are you from originally?"

"Pennsylvania, the western edge. Is there a reason you want to know all this?"

She sat up. "Consider it an interview. Not that I'm saying I've agreed to your offer, but part of the deal was that I'd know who the baby's father was."

He'd been in situations where controlling his reactions meant saving his life. He concentrated like hell on controlling them now. "You're considering it?"

"I'm not sure I like what I'm hearing."

He sat up fast, unsure whether that stabbing sensation near his heart was a bad rib or a jab at his pride. "What's wrong with it?"

"You're alone too much."

"That's part of my job."

"And the job is all-important."

"Doing the right thing is. You disagree?"

"Not with you. I just don't see how your ex-wife could have overlooked what a dedicated, honorable man you are."

He grunted. "Dedicated, honorable, and never around. She said I loved the job more than her."

"Did you?"

He didn't answer, wondering what the hell he'd gotten himself into. It had been a straightforward proposition; he hadn't planned on airing every piece of dirty laundry. "I wasn't cut out for the typical nuclear family."

"Or she wasn't cut out for you."

"I don't blame her."

"That's apparent."

"What does that mean?"

"You fail in one relationship, and Lord knows so many marriages don't last nowadays, and poof! You give up."

Poof hardly covered it. "We've had this conversation. There's a right way and a wrong way to be a husband and father. Both require being there."

"Tell that to long-distance truck drivers and off-shore oil riggers and overseas military men. They can love their families just as much. So Carla wanted a stay-at-home husband. That doesn't mean you were a failure."

"The divorce decree did."

Plain and simple. Black-and-white. Bridget fumed quietly and got up. She tugged the cloth out from under him, flapping twigs and grass off it before folding and stuffing it in the basket. "What about living life the way it is, taking what comes, being appreciated for who you are and not what you're supposed to be?"

"So this is her fault?"

"If she had any sense at all, she'd have held on to you come hell or high water." *I know I would.*

ELEVEN

Bridget hummed Johnny Rivers's "Secret Agent Man" all the way to the sandy beach. Narrow, barely discernible trails wound through the trees along the bluff. At points they were nearly level with the lake. At others they looked out over it. Or she did. A hundred yards behind her Ben trudged on, refusing to rest or slow down. He needed to do things for himself. She desperately needed a few moments' solitude. She paused out of his sight, listening to his ragged breathing and an occasional frustrated curse when his leg pained him.

Her breathing wasn't too steady either. Her body trembled and her heart reeled at what she'd almost said back there at the granite clearing. *I would hold on to you.* What next, an outright declaration that she feared she was falling in love with him? Or the admission that she already had?

If it wasn't love, what excuse did she have for what had happened next?

She sat and waited for Ben to catch up, remembering the last half hour. She'd tried discussing his offer impartially, giving it the careful scrutiny she'd afford a building plan or retreat layout. It wasn't making love, it was getting pregnant.

Ben didn't see it that way.

"We're getting off the subject," she'd said.

"We haven't been on it yet. Last night you couldn't keep your hands off me."

"I needed someone."

"You came to me."

"All I wanted was a hug."

"All you did was touch me damn near everywhere. If you want to talk about it, let's talk. You know it's bound to happen eventually."

"You're awfully confident."

"It's like a storm in the air. It's coming. I say we put it to good use. You want a baby and—"

"And you want no responsibility beyond fertilizing an egg."

"I wouldn't put it that way."

She wouldn't either. She didn't believe he could make her pregnant and walk away, not without damaging his soul, cutting out a piece of his heart. The man was as responsible as Eliot Ness.

"If the best in modern science didn't work, who's to say it'd work this time?" she hedged.

"If not this month, maybe next."

"And if it's not long enough?"

"I could make a terrible joke about that."

Sitting on the rock remembering, she stifled a smile. His humor always caught her by surprise.

"Who knows if once would do it?" she'd said next.

"Who says it has to be once?"

Even remembering, her skin tingled and she felt

too warm, edgy, and restless. She paced the top of the bluff. Ben had almost reached the top. She called to him that she was going on ahead, all but running to the sandy beach.

"I don't have any diseases if you're worried about unprotected sex," he'd said. "We get pretty thorough physical exams, HIV tests, all of it."

"Can you make it any more clinical?"

"What could be more clinical than you and some doctor?"

"It's so unromantic."

He combed an errant strand of hair off her forehead where the wind toyed with it. "Is that what you want? Romance?"

"No."

"Are you sure?"

Her heart felt as tossed and blown as her hair.

He'd traced her cheek, her mouth, the lashes of her closed eyes. "You want this to be love, not sex. Is that it, Bridget?"

Yes. The word echoed through her, a silent cry he'd never hear.

She turned from the water's edge and watched him step out of the woods into the sunlight. Like a pirate, his black hair glinted. Perspiration sparkled on him like ocean spray. He'd rolled up his sleeves. She thrilled at the thought of being held in those arms.

"You didn't tell me we were hiking the damn Andes," he groused.

"The Porcupine Mountains. You said you wanted to search for footsteps."

"Foot*prints.*"

"Kidding."

"I'm going to scan the perimeter."

"You do that." She turned back to the water while he walked the tree line. She couldn't do it. She didn't have the nerve to take him up on his proposition. It *was* too clinical; there were too many risks.

What happened to seizing life? a small voice taunted her. She could have a baby without a man, but she couldn't have sex without love.

No, she realized. The problem was that she couldn't take love and not give it. It had to be a two-way street. Ben, in his lonely determination to do right, thought he could give her a miracle, a life, and ask nothing in return.

She was a healer in her own special way. She built retreats for people who needed to step back and see what really mattered. She'd do her best to make him see it too.

She filled her lungs with the crisp scent of cold water. "Find anything?" she called.

"Deer prints. No sign of people."

"Then we're alone."

He walked a step farther, then slowed and looked her way.

It was up to her. Sand shifted beneath her feet as she walked to him. "You should rest," she said, her voice unexpectedly husky. "You've been limping since we stopped for breakfast."

"It'll pass."

She smiled knowingly. "You're being tough."

"If I whine about a little pain, who knows when the warden will let me out again?"

"You can go anytime." It was one of the things that frightened her.

"I'm not gone yet."

Then it was settled. She took his hand and led him to the tawny center of the wide beach. "Sit down."

He lay back, balancing himself on both elbows. She knelt beside him, taking off his shoe, then his sock, then the other shoe.

"What's this for?"

She bent his toes one by one, her thumb stroking his instep. "According to Richie, foot massage is a natural painkiller." From the way his jaw clenched, she'd never have guessed. "Didn't know it could feel so good, did you?"

His silence let her words echo in the air. "It could get even better."

She shushed him. "I have to get you back to the lodge. To do that, you have to walk."

"Why?"

She laughed. "Because I can't carry you."

"I meant what can we do there, we can't do here and now?"

Her hands' kneading motion kept the tremors from showing. She worked her way up, stroking his heel, his Achilles' tendon. Moving up his calf, she kneaded the underside of his knee. He bent it, surprised at how sensitive the area was and how persistent his masseuse could be.

Ben narrowed his eyes. What was she up to, ministering to him like this? His limp had gotten progressively worse. She probably felt sorry for him. Probably thought the poor sap couldn't get it up if he hired a hoist.

He glared at the blue sky, folding his hands securely behind his head. "Wake me in ten minutes. We'll head back."

"Anything you say," she cooed.

He peered out of one squinted eye. The sun was nearly overhead. He let it warm his eyelids. A shadow passed over. Her lips brushed his. Rigid as a slab of shale, he stayed put. "What was that for?"

"A test."

"Of my willpower?"

"Of mine." She ran her wicked hands along his arms, the contour of his collarbone, the swell of his chest.

"Bridget."

"I'm thinking."

Apparently she thought with her hands. Hands-on, that's how she'd described it. All he had to do was endure.

She returned to massaging his leg. The right thigh was overworked and shaky, the left underused and aching. She took pains not to come too near his wound. Running her hand above it, she stroked the place where his hip flexed. Her fingers curled around his thigh.

The sun beat down. Waves sluiced onto the beach. He glided her hand to the safety of his abdomen.

"Nurses have discovered that touch makes people heal faster. Did you know that?"

"Am I the one who needs healing?"

She nodded, her gaze level with his. "You're a wonderful man. You made one mistake and never gave yourself a chance to make another."

"Giving you a baby wouldn't be a mistake."

"What do I give you in return?"

"I don't need anything."

"Or anyone?"

"Don't make this more than it can be."

"It takes two, as the saying goes. I want to give you something."

He lowered his arms and bumped her wrist toward the center. She accidentally skimmed the bulge to the left of his zipper. Her hand stalled.

"I was wondering how long before you noticed," he murmured.

She surprised him. She grazed her hand across the fabric, her fingers sensing his heat. "I meant what I said about giving you something." There was more than one way to show love.

It had made sense at the time. Bridget crunched a carrot a week later, mortified at her powers of rationalization. At the time she'd felt like an angel of mercy, giving Ben just a fragment of the kind of love he offered her. She'd kissed him with no hesitation or modesty, as if every inch of him was something she treasured. His smoldering look had made her feel like the sexiest, most powerful woman on earth.

He'd stopped her at the last minute.

She didn't know if it was the incompletion or her blatant seduction that had them both on edge and wary. In the past week she found herself unable to pass him in the hall without averting her eyes, or worse, making hearty small talk about the weather or the waves or which room she had redone that day.

Embarrassed self-consciousness might explain her nerves. More frustrating was Ben's pleased reaction. Since that morning he seemed to think he had every right to kiss her when she stopped by to say good night, to touch her when he came downstairs to share her breakfast, to spend time with her during the few hours when their schedules overlapped. His arm curved regularly around her waist. His nose nuzzled her hair as if he'd done it a hundred times and planned to do it for a lifetime more.

The night before he'd sat with her by the bedroom fireplace, glowing coals taking the chill off an Upper Peninsula cold snap. He'd spread kisses the length of her neck, buried his hand in the shadows at her nape. Like every other amorous encounter, he'd taken it no further, although every square inch of her body screamed in frustration. If he meant to go through with it, when?

Bridget snapped off a piece of celery, slathering it with cream cheese. He could be so gentle, so intense, so loving. Could a man really hold her the way he did if he felt nothing? And what about all those questions? In the last six days he'd asked about her job, her family, eliciting opinions on current events and debating them. They'd butted heads on almost every issue and had had so much fun, their friendship was becoming as vital to her as their love.

Her love. She had no idea what his opinion was. All she could act on was what she'd observed—his honor, tenderness, protectiveness, desire. The man was either a walking Superhero or seriously interested.

But love? She sat at the table, head in her hands. She wanted his love. But the closer it got, the more frightened she became. She reread the grocery list he'd given her that morning. Strange to think anything so mundane could send her into a panic.

But these weren't just any groceries. He wanted steaks, two of them, at least an inch thick. He wanted red wine, a good one, and red-skinned potatoes. He specified herbs and garnishes, sour cream. He'd said she'd done enough cooking for him; it was his turn to cook for her.

"A great liar to the end," she murmured. From his gruff manner and romantic menu, she suspected he was planning a lot more than cooking tonight.

Driving the Jeep over the rutted two-track driveway, she turned onto the blacktop and headed north toward Copper Harbor. A gust of wind blew the list onto the seat. She swerved to retrieve it, then swerved back. Funny, she thought. She was holding her future in her hand, written out in black-and-white. She could always ignore it. Thank him for his concern and turn down his offer.

She pictured his carefully shielded response. An undercover agent to the last, Ben never let his feelings show right away. He'd argue. He'd ask why not. He'd listen to whatever reasons she gave and let her decide.

"No thank you, I don't want you in my life. I don't find you father material." She'd never say that. But that's what he'd hear. He was proposing to love her, not for all time, not in sickness and in health, but as much as he was capable of. If she chickened out now, he'd get the message she didn't think he was worth loving back.

Passing the rust-spotted gray hulk of a deserted mine shaft, she knew better. Proving it to him, then letting him walk away, would be the hardest part.

Pulling into a space before the tiny grocery store, she paused in the entranceway. Beneath a bulletin board filled with notices for snowmobile repair and cottages for sale, she found the pile of old newspapers by the recycling bin. She thumbed through the previous weeks' editions until she found the article about the unknown hunter found dead in the woods. She read the article until the words swam, shuddering at how impersonal they sounded; how real they might have been.

She remembered the rain on the night Ben appeared on her doorstep. The booming knock echoed in her mind, the color of his blood blackening his slacks, pain clouding his eyes. He'd silently implored her for help. She hadn't failed him then, how could she fail him now?

Wrenching a cart from the line, she strode up and down the aisles. Nose in the air, she breezed by the cigarettes. The diaper aisle slowed her steps. Baby food. Bottles. Wipes. So many details she'd have to see to. Alone.

She straightened her shoulders. She'd have Ben. In her memories, in her child. She could live with that.

Or could she? Bridget pulled the Jeep onto the shoulder, the grocery bags jostling in the backseat. "Decision number two hundred and three. What's it going to be?" Usually she made no bones about talking to herself. That way she never lost an argument. She was losing this one.

Where did Ben Renfield get off giving up on married life because *he* didn't live up? It was his conservative attitude, those maddeningly high standards of his that drove her nuts. He wasn't cut out for an Ozzie and Harriet universe. Who was? Life was riotous, disordered, chock-full of liberal abundance. "Take babies, for instance. Do they live according to rights and wrongs? They don't even know what *should* is. They just are."

She pictured him shaking his head, infuriatingly tolerant. More than once their debates had ended in kisses, sweet searching caresses that stopped just short of lovemaking. He was making her crazy when all she wanted was to make him see.

A bag of sinfully caloric goodies called to her from the backseat. She turned directly left, taking a narrow path into the woods. Overgrown branches scraped the Jeep's sides as she barreled farther down the muddy two-track. This should be the outer edge of the lodge's acreage. She'd explore, survey, map it out. And she wouldn't go back to the house until she made up her mind.

Good thing you brought dinner—her conscience sneered—*you'll be out here for months.* "Oh hush."

Suddenly something caught the corner of her eye. She eased off the gas. The engine whined as she put in the clutch. In a fern-filled clearing a couple of stone foundations and a pair of charred tilted beams betrayed an old logging camp.

She hopped down from the idling Jeep, listening. A path flattened the ferns to a padlocked tar-papered building. A deserted deer camp? Somebody's snowmobile storage?

A woodpecker hammered a faraway tree. Leaves rustled. There was something eerie about the spot. It was deserted but recently visited. Waiting.

She turned back to the Jeep. She had a crowbar in the back. It'd come in handy for breaking that lock. It *was* the lodge's property. What if she found contraband? "They're probably smuggling pot," she mumbled, the kind Richie used to ease the side effects from his chemotherapy.

A twig snapped. She froze. Backing up slowly, the forest whirled in slow motion as she turned three hundred and sixty degrees. She listened to her heels crush dried leaves. The road out had been blocked by a downed tree—recently cut, she realized. She could almost hear a chain saw's violent whine.

Something moved. She leaped into the Jeep, threw it in gear, and gunned it. Jumping the downed tree like the speed bump it was, she careened down a path that could only lead to the lakeshore. The white tail of a deer flashed in her rearview mirror. It didn't matter. Nothing could make her go back the way she'd come.

A branch slapped the windshield. She nearly sideswiped a sapling. Paranoia met hysteria. "Damn you, Ben Renfield. Somehow this is all your fault!"

Ben paced the tower. He toed the throw rugs. He slammed open the bedroom door and marched up and down the hall. He didn't bother looking in the bedrooms. Not this time. She hadn't been there since he'd woken up at three. He'd sent her grocery shopping. Hadn't she promised to come right back?

Not that he recalled. Bridget was independent to the core. Perhaps she'd come back and gone out again. There were no fresh groceries in the refrigerator. He'd checked. Twice.

Where else would she be? Not traipsing around the damn countryside. They'd argued about her map making a couple nights before. "I *have* to have a layout of the land so we can design nature trails," she'd said.

He clenched his fists as he remembered what he'd

said. In slow-motion replay he heard his usual pomp-ous, dictatorial self telling her in no uncertain terms she was to stay out of the woods.

"I walked those woods for two weeks before you got here. I never got in trouble then."

"If you got hurt now, it would be different."

"Why?"

Because it would be his fault. He was there to pro-tect her. "Is that what you're calling it?" he asked himself wryly, checking out the parking space behind the house. He was getting possessive, obsessive, bossy. He acted as if he owned her when he'd never even said he loved her.

She hadn't said it either. So much for words. He'd noticed the sparkle in her eyes every time she saw him, the animation when she told him events of her day, something funny Richie had said on the phone. She didn't back down or fade no matter how many times he pointed out his failures and shortcomings. The woman was in love with him.

The look in her eyes when he touched her con-firmed it. The heat in his blood pressured him to pur-sue it. But the future held him back. What happened when all was said and done? Did he just walk away? Another failed and absent father? Another AWOL lover?

She'd planned on raising the kid alone anyway. Not that that absolved him of anything. A man had responsibilities.

I notice she hasn't asked you to stay on, his conscience countered. How could she? He'd made it clear he was there temporarily. He'd kept her rigorously on the far side of a line drawn between them, between family and career, desire and duty. He could make her pregnant, if they were lucky, but he couldn't make any commitments.

So is there some reason you've been searching this coast for the last hour for a glimpse of her? He raked the telescope up and down the shore. He'd opened every west-facing window so he wouldn't miss the sound of her car driving up. Worry tied his stomach in knots and shot acid through his veins. If that wasn't love, what was?

Suddenly a piece of glass glinted on the bluff four miles north. He zeroed in, twisting the lens into focus. The black-and-white sheriff's car sat in a clearing overlooking the water. When a figure stepped out of the car the sideview mirror deflected the afternoon sun Ben's way. Or was it a signal?

He swung the telescope toward the lighthouse at the other end of the bay. No answering signs. He swung it back just in time to see a shape move through the forest toward the car. He cursed the trees blocking his view. Stonesmith had told him they'd needed the sheriff's cooperation to plant the story about the dead hunter. The sheriff had been "privately informed," Carville said, instructed about an injured agent "removed from the scene." Maybe, after that little scare, the smugglers were finally coming out of hiding.

Another flash of light. Another car door opening.

Ben's heart clogged his throat. It was Bridget. She jumped out of the camouflage-green Jeep and walked up to the sheriff. Ben watched her swing her hair to the side, capturing it in one hand so the wind wouldn't whip it. She wasn't a conspirator, he'd stake his life on that. She was probably lost, asking directions.

"Don't trust him," Ben shouted.

Peering through the scope, he gritted his teeth.

Bridget not trust someone? She'd exhibited that character flaw the first time she'd let him in. She probably treated everyone the same way. In which case she could be in big trouble.

What would he do about it? He loved her, dammit. Loving her was the only thing that explained why he stood there, throat dry, lungs hollow, not moving a muscle until she got in her car and drove back into the woods.

The sheriff didn't follow.

For the first time in what seemed an eternity, Ben breathed again. He loved her. What the hell was he going to do about it?

TWELVE

"Smells scrumptious."

He stared at the pan, flipping the sautéed onions with an expert flick of the wrist.

"Never could do that," Bridget tried again. He'd been withdrawn and tight-lipped from the moment she'd driven up. As he'd stalked outside to help her with the groceries, she'd noted his glower and expected a tongue-lashing. Instead she'd gotten a heart-racing, back-bending kiss that had left her dizzy and wobbly for minutes. By the time the earth had stopped spinning under her feet, he'd filled his arms with grocery sacks and headed into the house. Since then, barely a word had passed between them.

Before they ate she wanted to find out what was eating him. Her day hadn't exactly been a picnic. She'd returned to the lodge ninety-nine percent determined it was her job in life to convince this man he was worth loving. As for loving him back . . . the emotions were easier than the act.

When he'd handed her the list she could have

sworn the smolder in his eyes meant he'd intended to cap off their evening with an unforgettable night in bed. His welcome-home kiss had curled her toes. He'd asked her to find candles for the table and turned up his nose at anything less than the lodge's best china. He was throwing a mouthwatering dinner together as if he were a seasoned chef and laboring over it like a doting mother. She would have sworn it was for her sake, but his distant, preoccupied manner made her doubts rise. The nerves she'd contended with all day wound their way through her emotions like tangled electrical wire. One bad spark and the whole evening could go up in flames. If it hadn't suffered a meltdown already.

Ben flipped the onions one more time.

"I'm such a klutz they'd end up all over the stove if I tried that." Bridget laughed. "They did once."

"When was that?"

Encouraged, she smiled. She'd get him to do the same before this meal was done. "I was making dinner for a boyfriend—actually it was breakfast, he'd stayed over—"

Bad move; Ben's expression turned to stone.

"Anyway"—she spoke faster—"the next morning I was trying to impress him with my domestic abilities, so I tried making him breakfast. When he walked into the kitchen I tried saying good morning while flipping a pancake. The underside was done, it was golden brown, but the top was still batter. Guess which side ended up adhering to my chest? I still remember it sliding down—"

He laughed and shook his head, spearing a steak with a long fork and laying it on the layer of onions. "You're something else."

An ambiguous statement if she'd ever heard one. She covered her nervousness by straying to the table. Thoroughly befuddled, she hummed, poking through the half-emptied bags of groceries, putting away what she could. When she stood on tiptoe to put the tomato sauce in the cupboard beside the stove, Ben snaked out an arm and caught her around the waist. Their hips bumped.

"What's that for?" she asked playfully, bumping him back.

"You've been rushing around since you got home."

"And you've been very quiet. Do steaks require that much concentration?"

He nodded—at the tenderloin. "I had a long day."

"Want to tell me about it?"

"Actually I was hoping you'd tell me."

"About what?"

"Where you were." He winced as he said it.

She wriggled around to face him and came body to body with his thigh. "Is that jealousy or just plain suspicion?"

"I trust you. It's the sheriff I don't know about."

Her mouth fell open. "How did you know?"

"I saw you."

She splayed her hands on his chest and pushed until she was two steps free and rocking back on her heels. "You were spying on me?"

"I watch the coast. You were on the bluff."

"I got lost."

"Exploring again?"

"I was trying to find a place to sit and think about you. And me."

"But not what I said about the woods."

"The trail came out on the bluff and the sheriff was there. He knew an easier way out. It seemed safe enough. He asked if I'd seen any suspicious activity, teenagers partying, setting bonfires, that kind of thing."

"And you said?"

She looked at her distorted reflection in a spoon, wondering why she was lying to the man she loved. She didn't want him going to that camp, risking the life she'd just nursed back to health, a life that seemed to mean more to her than it did to him. The spoon clanged on the table. "I didn't tell him about you and I didn't mention the camp."

Ben turned from the stove. "What camp?"

"A deserted logging camp I came across. Everything was pretty desolate except the padlocked building."

"Are you serious?" He shrugged and turned back to his cooking. "Could have been a deer camp."

"That's what I thought. Probably nothing." She laughed.

"So where was it?"

Her blood turned thin in her veins.

He smiled gently, his eyes piercing blue. "Where, Bridget?"

"Approximately four miles north of our turnoff, maybe a mile in."

"Okay."

"Well, aren't you going to do something about it?"

He pursed his lips, musing over the golden onions ringing their steaks. "Think these are almost done?" He sliced one to reveal a light pink center.

She edged closer. "You're not going to rush out there and look for yourself?"

"It's almost dark."

"It was dark when you spied on them before." When he'd gotten shot, she meant. Her pulsed tripled.

He scraped onions over the steaks with a plastic spatula. "Wouldn't want to sneak up on our latest agent in the field. I don't relish getting shot by my own side."

"Then you're staying?"

He looked at her as if the answer were obvious. "We have some exploring of our own to do."

All the cooking aromas in the world couldn't fill the sudden airlessness in the room. They'd veered so far off the subject that had preoccupied her all day, it now loomed before her doubly intense and doubly scary.

Ben brushed a kiss over her lips. "I should have asked you how you liked it."

"Like what?" she breathed.

He canted his head toward the pan. "I like mine done on the outside, pink on the inside. If you don't like it that way, I can do it well."

A quivering started deep inside her, mimicking the sizzle in the pan. "I bet you can."

He grinned. "Then tell me how you like it."

"Make mine hot and bloody," her father would have said. She didn't dare. "What is it now?"

"Medium rare."

"Fine. I'm sure anything you do will be fine."

He winked. "I'll remember that next time."

Would there be a next time? This might be their only night. She reached for the wine bottle.

He got there first. "Let me."

She relinquished it, feeling awkward and out of place in her own kitchen. He'd taken over so matter-of-factly. He'd moved into her whole life as if he belonged there. He would move into her bed the same way. Once he had, he'd always be part of her life.

She watched him search through a drawer for a corkscrew, amassing mental snapshots, and letting her fears rule her. Live, remember? If life gave her only one night with him, she'd hang on to it with all she had.

He twisted the corkscrew into the cork. He'd conducted a search of the dusty wine cellar while she was upstairs changing into her scoop-necked sweater and black stirrup pants. Considering the wardrobe she'd brought, it was the best she could do. He hadn't even noticed.

"Let's hope the cork doesn't crumble," he murmured as he worked. "I had to cut my way through the cobwebs with a machete. Indiana Jones in the Temple of Wine. I expected a giant bowling ball to roll after me the minute I lifted this sweetheart. Nineteen-nineteen. The year not the price. The Dodges knew their stuff."

"I don't know about 'borrowing' seventy-five-year-old wine from the cellar."

"Your company owns it now."

"I'm supposed to do an inventory."

"Then it will be minus one bottle."

Her skittering pulse grew mysteriously still as she watched his hand grip the neck, his wrist thick and tanned. "I don't know if I'm hearing right. Did you just say something less than ethical?"

"When it comes to wine, and women, I have my moments."

He did indeed. The cork popped with a soft thudding sound. He slid it reverently out of the bottleneck, its tip dark with red wine. Tapping off a drop, he set it on the counter. A whiff of wine reached her, heady and suggestive. He never stopped surprising her. She tried to imagine life with Ben Renfield in it and closed her eyes against a quick spasm of pain.

"Smell vinegar?"

"What?" She looked up.

"Not all wine ages."

And not all love lasts, she thought.

He poured his own glass first, then saluted her. "Just in case." He watched her over the rim as he sipped. His lips turned dark and moist. His tongue swept over them. He savored the wine on his tongue, his gaze lowering to her mouth. "Magnificent."

For one silly, unreasonable second she thought he meant her.

He lifted the glass to her lips. She drank the rich old wine. Its aroma alone was enough to make her head spin.

"Taste good?" he asked.

She didn't have the heart to tell him. Anticipation made everything taste faintly tinny. The wine rested on her tongue, slowly permeating her senses with its own seductive power. "It's wonderful."

"That's just the beginning." His gaze fell to her lips. "More?"

"Please."

Neither of them moved. Just when she was sure he'd cover her mouth in a breath-stealing kiss, and that dinner would be forgotten, he poured her a glass.

She held it in both hands. The red liquid coated the crystal.

"Same color as your sweater," he said.

He'd noticed. She lifted her glass.

"Wait," he said. "To us, to the meal, to the night. To watching the moon set and the sun rise. Together."

She clinked her glass with his and took a bracing drink. "I didn't know you were so romantic."

"You'll find out. Your hands are trembling." He nodded at the wine vibrating in her glass.

"I'm scared."

"So was I," he admitted, his expression flinty. "When I woke up and you were gone. When I saw you out there with the sheriff and couldn't do anything to warn you."

Suddenly her fears disappeared, banished in the need to ease his and repay his honesty. She set her glass down and wrapped her arms around his waist. "I was fine, Ben. I'm here, aren't I?"

He buried his hand in her hair, as if convincing himself that a handful of midnight could hold her there forever. "I didn't know that. I just knew I'd let too much time go by without doing what I said I would." He pressed her against the counter, his body hot and powerful against hers, so pliant and giving.

When the kiss was done Bridget remembered the world turning upside down the last time he'd kissed her the same way. It took even longer to settle this time. "That wine is going straight to my head."

He laughed, pressed her to him one more time, and twirled her toward the table. "Then let's eat. You sit, I'll serve."

She collapsed in the nearest available chair. He'd been scared? For her sake? Her head spun and her conscience scolded. He might stay another week, a month. If so, how many meals would they share? How many times would they make love? And by the time he left, how deeply and irrevocably would she love him?

Ben brought the rest of the meal to the table. Snapping a napkin open on his lap, he watched her thoughtfully slice into her steak. He couldn't remember the last time he'd sat down with a woman, talked about his day, asked about hers. Not that it had been a typical day. She wasn't a typical woman. How did you care for someone determined to make it on her own? How did he stop loving her when he couldn't pinpoint when it started? He'd knocked on her door and she'd let him in. She'd trusted him, although, God knew, he'd given her no reason to.

He went back even further, to the moment he'd seen her through the window. He'd hoped she could save his life. He still wondered about that.

"Ben?" She waved a hand in front of him. "Are you there?"

He'd never taken his eyes off her. "I'm here."

"Thinking about work?"

"Uh, yeah. I've got to make some calls after dinner."

"Oh."

He watched the emotions flit across her face as her gaze fell to her plate. He'd disappointed her already. He remembered the scenes whenever he told Carla he was going on assignment. He could have been away for weeks; this was only minutes.

"I'll clean up," she said lightly, making the best of it. Before she went, she rested her chin on her folded hands. "Great dinner."

"Do you like cooking?"

"Me? I do a good Salisbury steak, smothered in mushroom sauce."

"Good thing I cooked."

"I'm not that bad," she protested in mock indignation.

"I'm that allergic. Mushrooms give me hives."

"Aha. That's why you didn't know a morel from a Mosell."

He winced. "You're not going to let me live that down, are you?"

She grinned impishly. "Not when I picture those little mushroom trophies stuffed and mounted in dens across America. I laugh every time."

"At me."

"You know, I passed the cigarette section of the store today."

"Tempted?"

"It made me think of pot."

"Going straight for the hard stuff?"

"Seriously. Nicotine's addictive. Why is it legal when pot isn't?"

Why was she bringing this up now? He got the feeling she wanted him to know everything before they went any further, squeezing all the information she could into their limited time together. "Why is pot illegal? I suppose it's because it can alter your senses and impair your driving."

"So can smoking, if you drop a cigarette in your lap at seventy miles an hour."

"Anecdotal but glib. Typical liberal argument."

"Besides, marijuana can ease the side effects of chemotherapy."

He sensed she was getting to the real point at last. "Oh, that."

She bristled. "It works."

"The people who want to legalize it keep dragging out that old argument. Other things work just as well."

"Not on all people. If it was legalized for medicinal purposes—"

"It isn't. Until it is, it's breaking the law."

She sighed and blew out a candle. "My dinner with J. Edgar Hoover. I thought you were lightening up tonight."

"So what brought this discussion on? Your brother isn't—" He stopped himself just in time.

Bridget paused halfway to the sink. "Have you ever heard of the military policy regarding gays?"

" 'Don't ask, don't tell'?"

"You got it."

"In other words, I don't want to know any more about your brother."

She shook her head, an innocent look in her big brown eyes.

He remembered that sweetly indulgent smile from the morning she informed him about her pregnancy. She wasn't protecting her brother from him, she was protecting him from hitting the roof.

He drained the last of his wine and joined her at the sink. "Life with you would give a lawman ulcers, you know that?"

"Only if he's inflexible, unsympathetic, stubborn, and completely obdurate."

"Ob-what?"

"Obdurate. It means stubborn. I like saying it."

He set his plate by the sink. "Now she's researching ways to insult me. Should I be flattered or what?"

"Life happens."

"And rules are meant to be broken, is that it?"

"Bent. Occasionally."

"We've had this argument before."

"But never—" She glanced away.

He closed the gap between them. "Never on a night like this?"

She raised her chin, daring to the end. "I thought you'd want to know where I stood on the issue."

"I was more curious about how you lie." He gave her a soft kiss when she expected a hard one. She swayed into him.

"I wouldn't lie to you," she said, twining her arms around his neck.

His body throbbed, warmth coursing through him, transforming into compelling heat. "Maybe I mean 'lay.' Look it up next time you're in the dictionary."

At the moment she couldn't have found the *Oxford English* if all twenty-six volumes were laid end to end. She slanted her body the length of his.

He hated himself for what he had to say next. "Bridget, I really do have to make some calls."

She pouted, her lips pursed for another kiss. She laced a string of them down his neck. "Can't they wait?"

"I'll be back soon."

"Promises, promises."

He needed every ounce of willpower to let her go. But Stonesmith had to know about that padlocked camp, not to mention the mysterious appearance of the sheriff.

She swayed when he stepped away from her. Scanning his face, she turned abruptly to the sink. "If you want to work, go ahead."

He wanted to take her in his arms and tell her this

wasn't personal. If he did, it'd get very personal very quickly. "The dishes can wait," he said gruffly. "Why don't you go up to bed?"

She was hardly in the mood. "No, you go on. The portable telephone is in the great room. You can use it while I straighten up in here."

Bridget listened to his footsteps fade as she faced a pile of dishes. A simple task with a beginning, a middle, and an end was just what she needed. She filled the sink with hot water and a mound of bubbles that burst faster than balloons. Or romantic dreams. Doubts chattered and crackled in her mind.

He had to make a phone call. At this hour? What if her information about the camp was the final puzzle piece? Now they'd know where the smugglers had landed.

She tried to feel proud for helping him out. She only hated herself for helping him leave. She never should have told him. What was worse, there was something even more important she hadn't said.

If she could have rubbed the copper off the pot with a dish towel, she would have. He didn't have to stay. He didn't even have to love her back. But she'd be blood-boiling, floor-stamping furious if she failed to make him see what a good man he was.

She slapped down a squeaky-clean spatula and headed for the hall. He was talking in the great room. Hand resting on the massive door's iron handle, she waited. She heard the rumble of his voice and thought she picked up some tension, as if an argument was just concluding. Unfortunately, out-and-out eavesdropping was frustratingly useless with such a low-spoken man. She stomped back to the kitchen.

The room was as neat and empty as it had been

during the days she'd lived alone. Pushing the pearl-tipped button, she doused the lights. In the hall she turned down the chandeliers, leaving one table lamp burning so he could find his way upstairs. Halfway up she remembered the fire she'd laid in the grate in his room—but that was at the beginning of the evening, when she'd gone upstairs to change, searching for something romantic to wear, setting out candles around his bed.

Candles that would never be lit. There were things far more important to Ben Renfield; he'd made that clear from the start. Wanting more, for his sake, had been her first mistake. She wouldn't blame him if he'd completely changed his mind. She'd expected too much. Wished too much.

"Where are you going?"

She clutched the stair rail. "Bedtime."

He stood in the door of the great room, pressing the portable to his thigh. "It's not even ten o'clock."

"I did a lot of rushing around today. I'm tired."

She never could lie to him. A brooding frown drew his cheeks taut. He lifted the receiver without taking his gaze from her. "I'll call you back." He punched a button and set it on the table.

She looked down at him in the shadowy light. His hair was raven black, his features stark, strong, uncharacteristically subdued. The man had his doubts too.

"I'll be up in a minute," he offered.

All she had to say was no. The word caught in her throat. He'd made a lighthearted offer when she was curled in his arms weeping, another when they'd kissed and caressed on the beach. He was under no obligation to fulfill it. "You don't have to."

He trapped her hand against the rail. "I want to."

"Are you leaving?" She indicated the telephone.

"Not yet. Is that why you don't want to do this?" His hand slid off hers.

She ached to seize it back. Seize everything, her heart shouted. Not do this? She'd cherish the memory all her life.

She reached over the rail. He clasped her fingers and pressed her palm to his mouth, passionately, hungrily, his gaze smoldering when it met hers, capturing her in the turbulent shadows. "Do you like that?"

She never wanted to see those doubts in his eyes again. "It wasn't you, it was me. Nerves, I guess."

He came around the bottom of the stairs. Climbing one, he pulled her hips to his chest, swaying them both in a slow dance. "I'm not leaving until you know how important you are to me."

"I know that."

"Do you?"

She combed his hair back lovingly. "You risked your life trying to save me once."

"From the television."

"Maybe you were only delirious."

"I wanted to keep you safe. That's always been top priority."

"Safe isn't loved."

He mounted one more step, brushing the bangs off her forehead. "It's part of it."

The dance's silent rhythm stopped. "Is it?"

Ben knew what she meant: Is this love? "I never wanted to risk you being hurt because I came here."

"I haven't been."

"*I* don't want to hurt you."

"You think I can't handle this?"

He tipped her chin up, his mouth stealing a kiss. "Then why do you look so scared?"

She shrugged, pressing her breasts to his chest, their heartbeats matching in urgent rhythm. "Maybe because I love you too."

THIRTEEN

If she expected fireworks, she got them. He lit a match to the paper in the fireplace. The room blazed with a golden glow. One by one he lit the candles. When she shivered at the distance between them, he came up to her, a taper in his hand. Together they lit the vanilla-scented candles she'd stacked on the end table near the head of the bed. He wrapped his hand around her wrist, caressing the underside with his fingers as she held the trembling taper over the rose candles on the desk.

In the tower they lit the thin bayberry stalks on the table he used for his surveillance. She'd wondered if he'd mind. His answer was to move the telescope himself, the better to take her in his arms and dance. A draft from an open window made the flames bow and flutter. Their blended aroma added a muskiness to the crisp lake air.

Ben hummed, his cheek pressed to hers. Their reflections glided by on three sides. She marveled at how petite she looked next to him, and how protective and strong he looked bending to her. When he paused to kiss her, the tower revolved slowly behind her closed eyes.

Time and space dipped. He carried her to the bed. She refused to untwine her arms from around his neck, pulling him down with her. He tasted like wine. She wanted the salty warmth of skin. She unbuttoned his shirt.

He stretched out next to her before she got too far, dragging down the coverlet to pull out a pillow and place it beneath her head. He arranged her hair on its white case, patient, intent. When he saw her watching him, he cupped her cheek, his kiss lazy and deep. He wanted to do this his way.

Bridget let the heat build. She'd never known a man as giving. She told him so. He caressed her breast through her sweater. She told him she'd never felt as unselfconscious. She'd been so worried, but with him, she felt safe, free, right.

"Am I talking too much?" she asked, threading her fingers through his hair.

"You're wearing too much." He worked her sweater up to her breasts. Since he'd already tugged the wide neck off her shoulder, he seemed momentarily stymied about which way to go.

She stretched her arms overhead, her whole body overtaken by a languid desire to let him take the lead. The sweater came off. Candle flames flickered as Ben tossed it to the floor.

It had been a lifetime since she'd felt kisses through silk. His mouth was wet, hot, and hurried. She tugged her chemise free of her waistband, greedy to feel those kisses applied directly to her skin.

So sweet they hurt, tingles raced through her skin.

Ripples fluttered within her. Subterranean pools swelled inside her as if a stone had been dropped centuries ago, the undulating waves rebounding like echoes bouncing off a cavern wall.

She moaned his name. He'd spread his hands on her waist, his thumbs hooked beneath the waistband of her slacks. Reconsidering, he shook the hair out of his eyes and sat back on his heels. "Why don't *you* take them off?"

Gooseflesh rushed over her. The wispy breeze took intimate liberties with her naked flesh. She sat up. The candles' dim glow was nothing compared with the embers in his eyes. She remembered the way he'd watched her when he was in pain, the way he'd needed her to be there, to not let go. The intimate connection was about to be consummated.

She curved her legs off the bed and stood. A layer at a time, she peeled down the black stretch pants, then the short black socks. Lastly the tiny triangle of lace-trimmed silk fell from where it hugged her hips. Silk showed moisture. She saw Ben's gaze fasten on the damp spot.

He got off the bed. She expected him to take her in his arms, to align his body with hers. He stood apart. She'd gotten so used to the old-fashioned clothes he wore, she barely noticed the suspenders. She watched him shrug himself free. His wide blunt hands unbuttoned the five buttons on his fly. Her temperature rose as he worked his way down. At the bottom he fished out the hem of his white cotton shirt, which he unbuttoned from the bottom up.

As the shirt parted she glimpsed his white boxers, the arrow of hair above his navel, the leftover smudge of a bruise by his healed rib, his dusky brown nipples.

She'd seen his body before, mud-streaked and scratched. She'd seen him look at her with banked desire. She suddenly found the air thready and hard to breathe.

He stripped off the shirt. It dropped at his heels as he stepped closer. She heard the waves outside, their roar blending with the blood pounding in her ears. He reached for the hands hanging limp at her sides and led them to his waist. The next move was up to her.

She eased the roomy slacks down. They fell with no more sound than the froth of waves absorbed by sand. Fitting her hand to his left thigh, she skimmed the hair on his leg, the thin white bandage that remained. He wrapped that himself nowadays.

"I've missed touching you," she said.

"I've wanted to touch you from the start." His fingertips grazed the underside of her breast. "To hold you against me. To see you like this."

"Can I see you?"

"Baby, you can do anything you want."

She grew bold. Reaching for the elastic on his boxer shorts, she spread it wide and worked it down. They dropped. He stepped out of them, eager to bring his body into total contact with hers. He nuzzled her neck, his lower body brushing her belly as they began another dance.

"We've got a lot of time to make up for," he murmured.

She didn't know if he meant the past or the future they'd never have. Missing him already, she kissed his hair, his temple, moaning in frustration when he kissed her breast and she'd wanted with all her heart to capture his lips with hers. He raised his head and gave her her wish.

"Your skin is like velvet," he whispered.

She moved in his embrace, wanting him to feel all of her. He filled his hands with her hips, his fingers digging into her flesh. She rose on her toes, the better to skim her softly rounded belly against his rippled abs. She shivered when his fingers trailed down the back of her thigh. He touched her more intimately.

Her skin burned with embarrassment, then flushed with desire. His guttural reply let her know he liked her responsiveness. His body seconded the motion. Honey-slick fingertips nudged her thighs apart. She raised her leg and wrapped it around him. Suddenly he lifted her, wrapping her around his waist, laving her breasts with hungry strokes, prodding her with a shaft of throbbing heat.

No amount of gentleness could disguise the hard power of him. He settled her on him, thrusting slowly, waiting for any sign from her. She clung to him weakly, her arms twined around his shoulders, her nails scoring his back.

"Hold on," he whispered.

Her body tensed.

He stepped to one bedpost, tugging down the gauzy drapes suspended from the rod. They fell with a puff of wind, as fluttery and insubstantial as she felt. He walked to the other side, dragging down another filmy barrier with arrogant impatience.

They hardly needed the privacy, Bridget thought. In a lodge on a shore overlooking the end of the world, they needed each other and nothing more. Laying her back on the bed, he thrust into her again, watching the candlelight gleam on her skin.

She wanted him closer, she needed him closer, deeper. He reacted to her every intake of breath, every intimate catch and cry. He drove into her until she arched to him, body quivering in exquisite anticipation. "Please," she begged. Clutching the muslin curtain, she cried in surprise when it tore.

He wouldn't let any distraction take her from him, not even for a fleeting moment. Cuffing her wrist in his hand, he stretched her arm over her head, kissing its velvety length. She raised the other to match it. He reared back, driving deeper, losing himself one more time in the cloudy desire of her eyes.

It was like lightning, Bridget thought, like shafts of electricity spearing the lake, striking without warning all across its surface, jagged and searing and powerful. That had been her climax the first time. She was too sleepy, and too content, to work out a metaphor for the other times.

She nestled her cheek to the pillow, looking toward the horizon and the pink glow growing there. She'd purposely put her bed where it was to see the sunrises. She'd never dreamed she'd share one with a man like Ben.

She felt him curled behind her, his body shaped to hers. Sometime during the night she'd curled on her side. He'd held her even then. She loved him for that, for the thoughtfulness he showed every time she'd rolled over and he'd been there to put his arm out and see to it she rested her head on his chest, or got the one pillow that hadn't ended up on the floor.

He'd pulled a quilt up over her barely an hour earlier, warding off the morning chill. She still felt the soft scrape of the fabric on her tender skin. He'd touched her everywhere until her body was exhausted, exhilarated, energized. She wasn't sure there'd been an hour of the night she'd slept all the way through, waking from time to time to look at him in the faltering candlelight.

What did it matter if she hadn't slept deeply? She felt deeply. She wanted to remember in the same way, to preserve this night on her skin, in her body, so these hours would never be lost.

He had the soul of a romantic poet and the merciless directness of a high-seas pirate. He'd had no compunction about driving her to the edge over and over, about making her beg. And demand. She'd told him what she wanted—when he hadn't guessed it from her pleased sighs. He'd granted every wish.

In the hazy early light her mind danced over their first time. She'd had very little time to treasure it. When she'd expected a delicious descent into shared sleep, he'd begun a slow massage beginning at her scalp and working its way down—her shoulders, her collarbone, a neck that had no tension left, tender breasts that learned anew how to tolerate then long for his touch, thighs that quivered from clutching him to her.

She'd been limp as a noodle, apologizing in a slurred voice for being so sleepy. The massage continued. Somehow, someway, sometime during his ministrations, her lassitude was replaced by low-level anxiety. Her toes clenched when he ran his thumbs across her arches. Lying on her stomach, she couldn't remain still when he worked the backs of her thighs. She wriggled, she fidgeted. Her hands itched to touch him back.

"Shh, let me," he'd said.

She almost believed it was her fault she couldn't

relax, her imagination that wouldn't stop picturing him kneeling astride her hips as he worked the muscles of her back one more time.

Then he kissed her spine. She grew breathless and still, aware it had only been an interlude. He lowered his body along hers. He drew her hair around the side of her neck, kissing the shell of her ear.

In the morning light, she rolled onto her back and stared in mute wonder at the dark angel who'd bedded her by firelight. He'd transformed himself once more to the earthy but indefinable Everyman who'd shown up at her door. That first night she'd thought he could pass for Italian, Greek, Mexican, Native American. No wonder he worked so well undercover.

She suppressed a grin. She'd have to tell him that one. She watched him sleep, a black lock falling across his forehead, his face relaxed but the jaw just as strong. He snored lightly. She'd have to tell him that too.

He probably wouldn't be surprised. She couldn't think of anything she could say that would surprise Ben. He'd shocked her during the night. More than once. She'd been pleased, stunned, and astonished at the responses he'd evoked from her, the openness with which she'd gone to him.

Later she'd awoken to find him crouching by the grate. Outlined by the red light of a dying fire, silhouetted before the massive stones of the fireplace, he looked primitive and powerful. He'd blown out the candles that hadn't guttered. The grate's stirred embers were all that was left to keep the chill out.

Until he turned and walked toward the bed and saw her watching him. "You're awake," he'd said.

One nod.

He reached for her. She knew the simple act of

taking his hand in hers would be a form of permission. She sat up, dragging the sheet with her. She knelt on the mattress's edge, kissing his chest, asking him for one more memory.

Was it the second time, or the third, when he'd said he loved her?

"What time is it?"

She glanced up. He automatically reached out so she could snuggle in the crook of his arm. "You can keep sleeping," she said, resting her wrist on his chest, fingering the whorls of dark hair.

"I've turned my schedule around. I'm used to being up all night."

She wrinkled her nose. "Puns? At this hour?"

He groaned. "That's not what I meant. Did I let you get enough sleep?" He snuggled her closer, kissing her hair.

Her heart swelled. She loved him for that.

"What are you thinking?"

Words she couldn't say. She turned her face before he saw the tears stinging her eyes. She hoped she could disguise the way her throat clenched. She'd cried in his arms the night before, an emotional release she'd been unable to subdue. He'd been loving then too. "I'm thinking I like being here," she said, her face toward the lake.

"The view is great."

She regained her composure and turned back to him. He brazenly scanned her bare limbs. "I could look at this view all day."

"You're a fiend."

"Just finding out?" He rolled on his side, the easier to trail his fingers over her abdomen. "I figured by now you'd be kicking me out."

She shook her head, her lips pressed tightly together.

"Say when." He brushed a kiss over those lips. He ran his hand over her flesh, admiring, desiring.

It was the possessiveness in his eyes that Bridget longed for and feared. He wasn't staying. If they were extraordinarily lucky, nine months from now she'd have a baby to remember him by.

She cupped his cheek in her hand. Babies rarely happened that easily. And men didn't always stay.

A cloud passed over his eyes. It humbled her when he picked up on her mood so fast. She thought she had good intuition. His fingers glided over the fine hair on her skin, the gooseflesh his touch produced. He'd told her he loved her during the night. In the light of day, he meant to show her.

It wasn't as consuming as the first time, or as exquisite as the second. Experience had become insight. He knew where to touch, how. His caresses seemed to start from inside her, shimmering their way to the surface of her skin. He stroked the honey-slick spot between her legs, and she shuddered to her soul and back.

He took her on a lingering, sensually charged journey, an exploration from which there was no turning back. No candles, no fire, no fireworks. He seduced her with words this time, *I love you*s and erotic praise and the prayerlike repetition of her name. He had memories of his own to make. If she was going to carry his baby, he wanted to leave her with all the love that went into making it.

❖━━━━❖

They were discussing whether to take a bath or a shower and who would be the unlucky one who had to get up and start the water when a slamming car door made them freeze.

"Stay here," Ben said. He got up without another word, stepped into his slacks, and padded across the hall.

Bridget was standing in the doorway when he turned from the window facing onto the drive.

"Stay here," he repeated.

"Who is it?"

If she thought she'd stop him by standing in the doorway, she'd better think again. He angled around her as if she wasn't there.

Torn between following him back to the tower room or peeking out the window, Bridget followed. "Who is it?"

"It's the sheriff." He snatched up his shirt, buttoning as he spoke. He nodded to her clothes.

She threw on whatever was nearest. "What's he doing here?"

"I called the agency last night asking for more background on this guy."

"He seemed very nice on the bluff."

"Your meeting him was the reason I called. If he was driving in that area he might have found the camp. Or else he was guarding it. Either way he knows I'm here."

"I didn't tell him anything."

"You didn't have to. I did."

"You what?"

"To plant that news article Stonesmith had to let the sheriff in on it. He knows there was an agent in the area. I suggested the agency call and arrange a meeting—*tomorrow*."

"You wanted him to come here?"

"I wanted him to head this way so I could meet him on the two-track. I didn't want him knowing you were involved." He shoved his arms into a T-shirt and pulled it on. "He's a day early. Heads are gonna roll."

Bridget pitied the person who'd screwed up that little detail. "What are you going to do?"

"Go downstairs and say hello." His casual tone belied the steel in his voice a second ago.

"Can you trust him?"

"I can't hide in here."

It didn't sound like such a bad idea to her. She searched everywhere for her other sock.

"They were supposed to call him at seven A.M. Assuming they screwed up by twenty-four hours, he got the call twenty minutes ago." Thinking out loud, Ben stepped into his shoes. "That means he got here damn quick from Calumet."

She hopped into her loafers. "Is that good or bad?"

He stayed with the good. "If he's with the smugglers, it could mean he had no time to marshal them. He decided to check me out on his own."

"And if he's honest?"

"The agency told him we'd need him in on the bust. He could be here to introduce himself."

"Why rush to do that?"

"Good point."

"Maybe he'll just pretend he's on your side until he can get the drop on you."

His smile didn't reach his eyes. "You're beginning to think like an agent."

She didn't feel like one. Her head spun and she still hadn't jettisoned the hiding idea. She had on one sock and shoe. She held the other shoe helplessly while she scanned the room for that AWOL sock. "What can I do?"

"Stay out of the line of sight and do everything I say." With that he slipped across the hall. By the time she caught up Ben was craning his neck to catch another view of their quarry. The sheriff, a young man in his late twenties, stood beside his car, scoping out the area. He pushed his sunglasses up his nose and rocked back on his heels.

"He seemed so nice when I talked to him yesterday," Bridget murmured. Saying it again wouldn't make it true.

The sheriff surveyed the area, pacing off the north end of the porch, then the south. Finally he moseyed toward the front steps. Before he took them, he glanced up.

Ben tugged her out of the line of sight. "Let's go."

She followed him to his former bedroom. He reached under the mattress and pulled out the .45 Stonesmith had brought him.

The blood drained from her face. "You never told me there was a gun in the house."

"You didn't want to know."

As she headed toward the top of the stairs, the air seemed thick as molasses. No matter how close she followed, she couldn't seem to catch up to him. It was as if events were unfolding in slow motion. Bad sign, Bridget thought. Terrible sign. Real life did not work this way. Real life didn't crumble like dried rose petals in an old book. Emergencies, disasters, and tragedies happened like this.

And love lasted longer. It had to.

Ben grasped her elbow and led her down the stairs and along the hall. They stopped at the great room. Turning over pillows and cushions, he searched the sofa. "Take the portable phone and lock yourself in the wine cellar. If I'm not back in fifteen minutes, call the agency. Here." He'd found it.

The knocker boomed the length of the hall. Bridget jumped.

Ben hardly blinked. "Fifteen minutes."

She took the telephone from his hand.

"I'll wait until I know you're safe," he said.

She couldn't speak. She'd wait for him forever, but damn him, she wasn't standing by while he risked his life for law and order.

Pine needles rustled underfoot. Their crunch made her wince with every step. She put her hand out, fingertips scaling the lodge's sturdy exterior logs. Flattening her back to the corner wall, she studied the logs jutting out in a serrated stacked edge. She took a steadying breath and peeked through them.

Ben stood a few feet from the sheriff. The distance muffled their words. The younger man's sunglasses cloaked his eyes. Ben didn't need props; his expression was entirely unreadable.

Bridget cradled the gun in both hands. She'd waited all of two minutes after closing the wine-cellar door. Punching in the number Ben had given her, she relayed a terse command for backup of any kind. Tiptoeing up to the kitchen, she saw light flooding the main hall. Ben had already opened the front door. He was out there talking to a man who might kill him.

Not if she was around. She grabbed a clanking ring of keys off a hook by the pantry door and padded quickly to the servants' room beyond the kitchen. Unlocking the rusty lock, she prayed the hinges wouldn't squeak. They didn't. Old Mr. Laatila had taken good care of this place. He took even better care of his hunting rifles.

Crouching outside minutes later, she blew the dust off the double-barrel shotgun and wiped her sweaty palms on her stretch pants. Not trusting her aim or her nerves, she rested the barrel's end on a jutting log. She aimed at the glinting silver star on the sheriff's brown shirt.

Her mouth tasted like the powdery sand beneath her feet. She felt as weak and willowy as the blades of yellow beach grass that sprang from the sandy soil. Adjusting her feet for balance, her heel scraped through the shallow surface to the granite ledge the lodge was built on.

Even through her terror she recognized the symbolism. It was a metaphor of love compared with emotion, the true bedrock strength that lay beneath otherwise shifting sand.

Thanks to a former boyfriend's skeet-shooting lessons, she knew how to load a cartridge in a shotgun. But the weapon only gave her two shots, and clay pigeons weren't human beings. She wouldn't do anything as long as the sheriff didn't draw his weapon.

Sweat trickled down her back. Details stood out. The day was cool, the early-morning light gray. A mist off the lake shrouded the woods, moving through them like ghostly deer. Ben's voice carried faintly.

"I've been conducting surveillance, primarily to the north end of the peninsula. . . ."

The sheriff's holster was strapped to his hip. He reached for it.

Ben's voice never wavered. Nevertheless Bridget sensed him stiffen ever so slightly. She stared at the .45 in his waistband. He wasn't reaching for it.

Her finger trembled near the trigger guard. The sheriff's hand moved past the holster to his back pocket. He pulled out a notebook.

Her sigh of relief emerged as a squeak. She clamped her jaw shut.

Ben's head moved slightly. She wasn't sure he'd heard her. Maybe that vein pulsed in his jaw for other reasons. He shifted onto one hip, took a step to his right, leaned that way again, subtly moving toward her corner of the house. He moved between her and the sheriff, blocking her view. She wanted to scream at him. Who was he protecting?

The young man tapped his notepad with a pencil. "If you should need any help," he said. Bridget heard paper tear. He handed his number to Ben.

Bridget wasn't buying the public-protector act. For all their muted conversation the young man seemed as distrustful of Ben as Ben was of him.

"And the lady of the house?" he asked with mock casualness.

Ben took another step toward the car. Their voices became clearer. "She went into town," he said. "Shouldn't be back for hours."

"I didn't pass her car."

"She headed for Houghton. Needed some kind of graph paper. She thought the college would have it."

The sheriff waited. Ben knew better than to over-explain a lie. The young man flipped the notepad shut and shoved it in his back pocket.

"We'd appreciate whatever help local law enforcement could give us," Ben said. He sounded completely at ease.

Bridget marveled at how he did it. Wearing suspenders, those old-fashioned slacks, and a scoopnecked T-shirt, he looked as disreputable as John Dillinger or Clyde Barrow rousted from a farmhouse hideout. Never turning his back on the sheriff, he circled around to the driver's side.

Polite but aloof, the young man picked up the cue to leave. Ben had come around to stand by the car's rear fender. Leaning on it with deceptive ease, he faced the house.

Bridget thought of signaling him with a wave. Then the sheriff swung open his car door. "No," she moaned. From where she crouched it blocked most of her view.

The sheriff leaned inside and reached for the radio mounted on the dash. "That should be all," he said with deceptive lightness. "Gotta check in with dispatch first. You wouldn't believe how she worries."

Out of the corner of her eye Bridget saw Ben nod. As the sheriff reached inside for his radio Ben stepped away from the car. He splayed his hand at his side, motioning her back. Her eyes locked with his. He wanted her out of there, now.

She shook her head. She wasn't the only one who needed defending. He glared. She tore her gaze away. She hadn't come there to be a dangerous distraction. She had to watch the sheriff. Any minute now all hell could break lose.

That minute arrived. One second the sheriff was reaching toward the radio, the next his hand veered to the shotgun mounted against the dash. Ben's arm jerked up in slow motion, his voice like a slowed-down recording. "Bridget, no!"

She never heard the gun go off. There was a puff of smoke, a deafening concussion, and she sat on her behind in the sand.

In the frozen split second it took to scramble to her feet and register what had happened, she saw the gaping mass of broken glass that had been the car's windshield. Ben had moved in a blur. He'd sent the sheriff sprawling across the front seat and dove in after him. As the air cleared, the passenger door flung open. The sheriff tumbled out the other side. Ben's outstretched arms pointed the .45. "Don't move!"

Bridget raced into the opening. Her ears felt stuffed with cotton. A high whine drowned out the sound of the lake.

Ben turned his chin very slowly in her direction. "And don't shoot," he added dryly.

She nearly dropped her gun. Stumbling to the car, she leaned it against the bumper. "Are you okay?"

"I'm fine," he said tightly. He climbed out, slamming the door so hard, the vehicle wobbled. His voice rose to the same decibel level. "Do you have any idea how easily you could have been shot?"

"You were the one in danger!" Her own voice rose to cover this buzzing hive of bees in her ears. "He was reaching for his gun!"

"You could've killed him."

"He could have killed *you.*"

"*I* could have killed you." He grabbed her by both shoulders. "When I'm standing here wondering who might come out of the woods, do you think I need you sneaking up behind me? You were supposed to be in the cellar!"

"And she seemed so nice on the bluff," the sheriff murmured. He climbed to his feet, swiping dust and shattered glass off his shoulders.

Dumbfounded, Bridget stared at both men. "Don't just stand there, point your gun at him! How do you know he's not with the smugglers?"

"Because he was going to shoot *you*," Ben said. He handed her the paper with the scribbled warning. *Gun behind you, NW corner.* "If he was with them, he wouldn't have warned me. I didn't know who the hell you were until I got a look."

She stared from Ben to the sheriff, then back again. "I feel sick."

Ben hustled her to the porch. She sat on the steps, a cold sweat breaking out everywhere. She needed to be held, to be comforted. Ben was too wrought up to comply.

"You shouldn't have left the house," he said, pacing before her like a schoolmaster.

The rest of the irate lecture was lost on her. Holding her head in both hands, she waited for the nausea to pass. A year of morning sickness would be preferable to this. She looked apologetically at the sheriff. "I'm sorry," she croaked.

He picked up her shotgun and broke it open, dumping the unspent shell on the ground. "I don't know how I'm going to explain that windshield. We aren't a big-city department, you know. These things cost money."

"You'll be reimbursed," Ben snapped.

Bridget gave the young man another weak smile. "You looked as suspicious of him as he was of you."

"There's been a lot of unexplained activity around here. I've been doing some surveillance of my own.

When I got that call this morning it dropped a lot of pieces into place."

"Dave talked to Stonesmith this morning," Ben explained. "They called him a day early so he could let me know the arrests were moving ahead. Immediately. I'm going with him."

"If I can drive without a windshield," the younger man groused.

"What?" Bridget wobbled to her feet.

"I have to go," Ben said.

FOURTEEN

His gentle voice did it. It got through where the exasperated lecture hadn't. He was serious. "You're going?"

"It'll take a day to get everything in place, then we move in on the American side and the Canadian side simultaneously. According to Dave here, agents will be arriving to set up a command post. Stonesmith suggested the lodge. It's a good way to keep you guarded."

She shook her head slowly. What they'd shared the previous night suddenly caught up with her. "You can't. We just— So soon?"

He stopped at the foot of the steps, his face level with hers. "I'll be back."

No, he wouldn't. She had no idea how dangerous it would be, but she knew he wasn't coming back. If he stopped by again, it would be to tell her the case was over, the surveillance finished, the perpetrators in jail. He'd come back to say good-bye. If he came back at all.

She turned toward the house.

He touched her shoulder.

She caught her breath against the pain. She'd saved his life so he could leave. She nodded at the aptness of it. Wasn't that how they had started out?

"Bridget." He came up on the porch, blocking the door before she could escape. He stood inches away. He didn't try to take her in his arms.

She silently thanked him for that. "You're going, then."

"I'll be back."

To say good-bye. He'd sworn to her once before that he wouldn't leave without saying good-bye. It was the only promise he'd ever made.

She looked up at him. For blue eyes his looked so dark. She blamed it on the deep shade on the porch when the morning sun hit the house from the other side. His eyes looked nearly black, his features unbearably stark. Uncertainty made his body breath-stoppingly still.

She wouldn't embarrass him with tears or humiliate herself with begging. "I guess we had our chance."

"I'll come back." He planted his fist on the door, waiting for her to say something, to argue.

She rose up on tiptoe and kissed his cheek, her lips barely touching it. "What you did was above and beyond the call of duty. You're a wonderful man. I don't know if you ever believed me about that. But I know I can't hold on to you. That's one thing you never lied to me about."

"Bridget—"

"For your honesty, I thank you. And maybe for more, who knows?" She patted her stomach.

He rasped her name again.

She shook her head, her hand gripping the door handle. "You have to go."

"Not until we settle this. I love you."

The words registered, then disappeared, like stones skipped over the lake. If she looked through the cold clear surface, she'd always be able to find them, to pick them up and examine them, then put them away until another summer, another walk along this particular shore.

"I love you," he repeated urgently.

She looked him calmly in the eye. "What good is that going to do me when you're gone?"

He cursed.

Touched, she pressed her fingers to his lips, silencing him, memorizing their faint curve. He wasn't taking this well at all. Just when she thought she knew him, he always surprised her.

"I loved you," she said. "Life gave me that. I can't stand here and demand life give me more, or that things have to end a certain way. This is it. We'll both have to deal with it."

She cleared the sand from her throat. "Meanwhile, you have very important work. Dangerous work. I don't want to be a distraction. If you ever got hurt because of me . . ." Her voice trailed off. She couldn't meet his eye anymore.

She was hurting him right then, and there wasn't a darn thing she could do about it. It was over. *He* was telling her that. But for some perverse, stubborn, inexplicably male reason, he didn't seem to want her to accept it.

She did. She had to.

❦━━━❦

I don't want to be a distraction.

Sitting in the woods listening to the rain slash the windows of the unmarked car, Ben heard Bridget's words. They mingled with Carla's voice the way the trees blurred in the driving rain. He remembered his ex-wife's sarcastic tone every time she referred to his "important work." Bridget had used those very words.

He squeezed the bridge of his nose, refocusing his tired eyes. Three in the morning, and they had yet to move in on the bust. He waited with another agent. The sheriff fought to stay awake in the backseat.

He'd told her he loved her, more than once. *What good is it going to do me when you're gone?* Bridget's words, Carla's sentiments. What good did it do to say he loved her if he was never around?

"So this is it."

"Huh?" The other agent turned to him.

"Nothing." *This is it.* Carla's words when she handed him the divorce papers. Bridget's when she touched his cheek and ran into the house.

He wished the crackle of radio static would break into some kind of "go." He needed action. He'd been out of commission nearly a month, sitting in that lodge, staring out windows. Falling in love.

If you got hurt because of me, she'd said. He'd been healed thanks to her. His heart had been twisted and broken and cracked wide open because of her.

He'd followed her into the house, convinced she wouldn't want him to and doing it all the same. "If I can't be back by midnight, I'll call."

They had both realized at the same time how normal that sounded, and how out of place.

She had played along. Stepping up to him, she'd straightened his suspenders where they'd become twisted. She'd swept her hands over his T-shirt, pinching the shoulders as if it were a dress shirt. Pain had clouded her eyes for just a moment. She'd let go.

Twenty hours later he refused to let go. At midnight he'd called just the way he promised. An agent answered; they'd moved in to set up operations and guard Bridget. Ben had insisted on that.

Apparently she'd insisted on someone taking her messages. He was tersely informed she'd gone to bed.

He pictured her in the tower room. Would she sleep with his pillow held to her body? Or change the sheets? Would the curtains drape lightly, or had she tossed them over the bar? Maybe she'd moved to her own room, deserting what had been theirs for one indelible night.

He took a sip of lukewarm coffee from a thermos. That would've been Carla's style not Bridget's. Then again, what did he know about women? He had nothing to offer her but a series of dangerous assignments and too many nights apart to sustain any kind of relationship. A couple couldn't build a marriage on one month of togetherness any more than they could create a baby after one night of lovemaking.

Unless they were very, very lucky, he thought. He wasn't feeling lucky.

He stepped out of the car. The lodge's dirt drive muffled his steps. Carville Stonesmith lowered his *Wall Street Journal*, rocking lazily on the big porch. "You moved in too?" Ben asked.

"Senior personnel," he drawled in his superior East Coast accent. "I believe she's on the bluff."

They'd known each other too long for Stonesmith's intuition to surprise him. He'd been scanning the house for some sign, a face in a window. It irked him to be so transparent.

He strode around the side of the house. He didn't ask which bluff. He'd find her. In fact, that was the whole point of his visit.

Half a mile south the bluff formed a steep sandy drop to the water. The rocks were piled high on the shoreline. She'd found one to lean against as she stared at the lake.

She didn't turn as he approached. "How am I going to know you're all right?"

He stopped, his shoes forming deep impressions in the wet sand.

She turned, arms folded, mouth set. "How will I know you're all right? You got yourself shot last time."

Ben angled toward the lake, hands in his pockets. He'd come to ask her to marry him, to argue with her, wear her down, insist. And to walk away a gentleman when she said no. Somehow she'd jumped two steps ahead, to how they'd actually live. "You could check in with the agency," he said.

"That runaround voice mail?"

"The real number. Stonesmith would be your contact." He didn't know why his heart was hammering so. Carla had had the same opportunities. She'd never adjusted.

Bridget considered it. "Stonesmith, huh? At least he didn't bring me a pack of cigarettes this time."

Ben waited.

She made conversation. "We've been getting to know each other."

Was that a veiled hint? He'd promised to call if he was out later than midnight. That had been four days ago. If she was mad that he hadn't talked to her since then, why didn't she just say so? He knew how to deal with angry. His threadbare defense went something like this. "I couldn't help it. We got stuck in the woods for a day and a half. The minute we rounded up the land-side crew we got on a powerboat for Canada. We chased them ten miles offshore. I even fired a shot across their bow. You would've liked that."

She laughed. Maybe the wind whipping the hair across her face tickled. She held it back.

He waited for the inevitable explosion. The *what about me?* The *I waited up. Where were you? I can't live like this.*

She shrugged.

He blinked.

She swung around to him and did it again. "Stonesmith told me there was a delay. It's your job. I understand."

He'd heard that before. Every other time it had been coated with frost. "You understand?"

"I just want to know who will be there if you get hurt? Who would take care of you, bandage you? Tell you you're loved?"

These weren't the questions he'd been expecting.

He scraped a hand over his cheek. His beard was beyond stubble. It had been a choice between cleaning up and seeing her that much faster. "Look, I can't change. I promised that before."

"Not to me."

"I know better. That's why I won't promise to change."

"Did I ask you to?"

No, but it was only a matter of time.

"Am I asking for nine-to-five and 'Honey I'm home'?"

He couldn't make heads or tails of it. Probably due to the four hours sleep he'd had in four days. He fell back on the speech he'd worked on in his few quiet hours. He'd say it, take her refusal like a man, then stagger back to his room.

"When I first came here," he rasped out, "I wanted to be sure no one hurt you. That's standard, routine. We're obligated to protect the public."

She tilted her head, studying him across the short distance separating them. "Have you been eating properly?"

Another crazy question. "No, dammit. I've been on stakeout."

She tsked. "I was wondering about that. What do they feed you out there?"

He didn't care. He stomped toward the exposed roots of a tree clinging to the bluff, then paced back. *She* was supposed to be the one in a snit. He'd pictured her spitting nails because he'd been a typical unreliable workaholic male who cared more for his job than he did for their relationship. Instead she kept asking puffball questions. She topped them off by stepping up to comb his windblown hair off his forehead.

"Now, what were you saying?" she asked lightly.

He started over. Good thing he had it memorized. It was practically engraved on his heart. "I wanted to protect you. Then somewhere along the line keeping you safe became keeping you happy. Then I wanted to give you the baby. I can still do that. I want to do that."

"So do I."

"If it doesn't take, I can come back. I could visit."

She huffed. Here it came, the anger, the hurt feelings. "That's not much of a proposal."

If she'd hold on a minute, he'd get to the proposal.

"Do you love me, Ben?"

Another query out of left field. "Yes." He'd loved her since she'd come to him in tears, since she'd slept in a rocker at the foot of his bed after working up the courage to let him in. "I don't know when it was exactly, but I somehow fell in love and it just won't quit. I loved you when I woke up with you the other morning. I loved you before that. Every time I think of you, or hear you laugh, or let you get my goat with all that liberal guff you hand out, I love you more."

" '*Let* me,' " she declared.

She was teasing. He was too damn serious to drag the inevitable out a minute longer. "I can't marry you."

She looked mildly surprised.

His ego could've used at least one tear. "I can't quit my job and get a job in some office, or follow you around from spa to spa while you design retreats for who knows who." He seized her shoulders in both hands as if she were life itself. "But I could find you, dammit. Anywhere you went, any project you took on. I could be there in a matter of days. I wouldn't be there every day. But I'd find you. I'd be with you every moment I could."

"Will you ever stop loving me?"

"No."

"Then all right."

What? She wasn't getting the picture. *Be there and do what?* she was supposed to say. *Stay a week? Or do I get two this time?* He had his answers ready even if her accusations were mysteriously slow in coming. "I couldn't stay long, but what would it matter as long as we found a way to be together?"

"You're right."

Of course he was right. He clenched his fists and scuffed the sand with his heels. "I know, I know. I know exactly how much it matters. You're independent, you've lived just fine on your own so far. But that doesn't mean you'd put up with my schedule forever. And forever is what marriages are all about."

She folded her arms over her sweater, shaking her head at the sad mess he'd made of things. "You want to marry me?"

"Just tell me to get lost and get it over with. I don't know why I came."

"Because you said you would."

He looked bleakly at her.

"You also said, just now, that you'd find me no matter how far apart we were, and come to me no matter how short the visit might be."

He nodded, emotion surging through him. "Nothing could keep me away."

"I believe you."

"You do?"

She smiled. Her eyes sparkled like sunlight dancing over the water. "I trusted you from the first time I saw you. I think I'll love you a lot longer than that."

She touched his face again, his throat, the lapel of the navy windbreaker a DEA agent had loaned him. "We'll have a lot of time to work on it, this love stuff." She rose up on her toes and kissed him. "Through the first baby." Another kiss. "And the second."

He held her waist in his hands, afraid he'd crush her if he clasped her to him the way he wanted. She wasn't big, his Bridget, but she was stronger than steel.

"I won't wait for you when you're gone," she said sternly, her small fists giving his lapels a tug. "I'll be too busy working and raising babies and planning what we'll do when you *are* home. Don't you expect me to be some sit-by-the-phone wife."

He couldn't imagine it.

"Promise you'll love me. That's all I need to know. As for the rest?" She shrugged. "The rest is life. We'll just have to take it as it comes."

If she could hang on to that, maybe they could make it, Ben thought. He kissed her hard, then soft, then he lost track of how. He kissed her until they lost all track of time. That was okay. That's why people in love had forevers.

EPILOGUE

One year later

Ben walked into the great room. Carville Stone-smith emptied his pipe on the grate, scraping the charred insides with a silver knife. "How's the trial going?"

"Four more days of testimony," Ben said. "Explaining international law to this jury isn't easy. I'm afraid I'm putting them to sleep half the time."

"I hear the women stay wide-awake."

"Bridget said they get that dreamy look on their faces and pay no attention at all to my testimony."

The room grew quiet when he mentioned her name. Both men stared at the dying flames flickering amid the uneven logs.

"Guess I'll head up to bed," Ben said.

"Good night."

He climbed the stairs. A cobweb on the antler chandelier caught his eyes. He'd have to mention it to the government housekeeping staff who'd taken over the care of the outpost for the duration of the Montreal-cartel case.

He passed the first bedroom, the one he'd stayed in those first few nights. He didn't need to see its white log walls. They were embedded in his memory. The second and third doors were locked. Tiny red lasers testified to the security installed to protect the stocks of documents stored inside.

"Renfield. How'd it go?"

"Not bad." He wasn't in much of a mood to make small talk with one of the other agents billeted there. Bridget's executive retreat had become a popular get-away for station chiefs and politicians interested in linking their names with drug enforcement. He doubted it would ever revert to its original use.

Then again, its comfort had led to a dozen commissions for Bridget. She hadn't told him about the "New Camp David" the President had requested. She didn't have to. He had his own sources of information.

But he didn't have her.

He walked into the tower, shut the door, and lit a fire. He stripped off his coat and tie, kicked off his shoes, and lay back on the bed. He'd known from the start they'd be separated for long periods of time. He'd never expected he'd be the one sitting home missing her.

He marveled at his injured male pride and reached for the telephone. She answered on the third ring. "How are you?"

"Just a minute."

He listened to muffled footsteps and the varying room sounds as she carried a portable from one place to the next. He heard a door shut softly.

"There. I'm in the bedroom." Her voice turned

sugary sweet. "How are you, little puddin'? Did you miss Mommy?"

He realized she was talking to their baby daughter. "Is she in her crib? Is she sleeping?"

"She's fine. You should see her."

"I'm looking at her." He'd reached for the silver-framed photo on the side table, Uncle Richie holding his namesake niece. "She's okay?"

"She adjusted to the time change wonderfully. She's almost sleeping through the night."

"What about you?"

"I'm doing okay."

She hadn't answered the question. Which meant she was probably up all hours. He didn't give her a hard time. He knew the reason. "How's Richie?"

"A little better."

A little better from pretty bad, Ben thought. He closed his eyes. "I'm sorry I couldn't be there. This trial is dragging on worse than the O. J. Simpson case."

"It's all right," she said.

He listened for the frostiness. It never came. In the busy year they'd had, she'd never once chided him for not being there. There had been his case and her commissions, his flights to Washington and hers to San Francisco, his reunion with his daughter, Molly, not to mention getting married and having a baby along the way.

"What are you thinking?" she asked, her voice right beside him despite three thousand miles.

"I was thinking I love you for all the things you *don't* say."

"Are you saying I talk too much?" she teased.

"You know what I mean. You never give me hell about not being there."

"But you are. You're here right now. You're here every time I think about you, or look at the baby, or put on that shirt of yours I packed."

He fingered the silk slip she'd left him under his pillow. He'd thought she'd forgotten to pack it. Crafty woman. She'd known he'd need the reminder. He lifted it to his lips. "I'll miss you tonight."

"I miss you every night."

He stared at the moon over the lake. "When are you coming home?"

"The end of the week."

Home. It was wherever their paths crossed, usually a set of rooms in her latest retreat or sometimes her Chicago apartment. He'd given up his apartment in Atlanta. But this was their favorite, Paper Birch Lodge.

He'd have to lay in a supply of candles. And bring up more logs for the fireplace.

"What are you thinking?" she asked again, her voice a low murmur that made his blood simmer.

He rubbed the scar on his thigh. "I was thinking how much I love you. How much I want to make love to you."

"I love you too. I'll see you in a couple days."

"I'll leave a light on for you." It was how he'd first found her. One light burning in a downstairs window. One woman. It was all he needed.

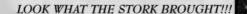

LOOK WHAT THE STORK BROUGHT!!!

NAMES: Meg and Chip
DATE: May 1, 1996
WEIGHT: Meg—8 megabytes
             Chip—6 microchips
PARENTS: PINK and Einstein

Special thanks to:

1st place—Carol Quinto for the
     name Meg A. Byte
1st place—Anne O. Ryan for the
     name Chip
2nd place—Carolyn Maxey for the
     name SKAMP (Super Kid
     Adored by Mega Prototypes)

Many thanks to all who entered the
"Name the Computer Baby" Contest. Turn the page for profiles of
our first place winners!

Carol Quinto lives in Deltona, Florida, with her husband, Mike, and two psychotic cats. Carol and her husband have been married for twenty years, and are still very much in love. An avid reader and true romantic at heart, Carol particularly likes contemporary romances (Loveswepts, naturally), Patricia Potter historicals, regencies, and mysteries. Fortunately, she shares the same tastes with her mother (who lives next door), so they are able to trade books. Both Carol and her mom are devoted fans of Einstein and PINK, and are thrilled about their new additions!

Anne O. Ryan and her husband of twenty-six years live in DeFuniak Springs, Florida, where they are the proud parents of seven children and four grandsons. Anne is an elementary school teacher, a volunteer for the PTA, Cub Scouts, Boy Scouts, and Little League Soccer, the secretary of the North Walton County Republican Club, and a member of her local Methodist church. Anne also loves to sew, crochet, and travel. And did we mention that Anne loves to read? Well, she does, voraciously, sometimes devouring as many as twenty books a week!

THE EDITORS' CORNER

Next month come celebrate LOVESWEPT's THIR-TEENTH ANNIVERSARY with a stellar lineup of your favorite authors, who prove that spooky thirteen, even the more chilling Friday the Thirteenth, can bring the best kind of luck. In each of their novels, the hero and heroine experience unexpected twists and exhilarating turns in their lives—and before they know it, they're swept away into the most passionate journey of all. So put your superstitions aside and join us next month on an exploration of the romantic power of thirteen.

Victoria Leigh casts an irresistible spell in **WAIT FOR MIDNIGHT**, LOVESWEPT #790. He usually draws people to him the way a magnet beckons steel, but attorney Ben Philips has never ached to charm a lady into his life as he does when he spies Kate Hendricks in her hospital flower shop. Stunned by unexpected yearning, Kate meets temptation with a tease—until she discovers Ben's ruthless interest in a mysterious patient she's taken under her wing. Victoria Leigh delivers tenderness and sizzle for a top-notch romantic read.

Praised by *Romantic Times* as "fascinating," the MAC'S ANGELS series by award-winner Sandra Chastain continues with **SINNER AND SAINT**, LOVESWEPT #791. Nikolai Sandor doesn't want to feel anything for the sleeping woman who resembles a fairy-tale princess, but only he can give Karen Miller a reason to live! Murmuring endearments, he tries to convince her they are more than strangers . . . until she awakens and begs her gypsy lover to make her fantasies come true. But can she forgive him for not promising forever? If you're looking for enchantment, then Sandra Chastain's beguiling novel is perfect for you.

Thrilling romance and breathtaking suspense ignite the pages of **PLAYING WITH FIRE**, LOVESWEPT #792, by Debra Dixon. Haunted by a long-ago secret hidden deeper than a dream, Maggie St. John can't brush aside the finger of suspicion arson investigator Beau Grayson points her way. He senses she knows more about the hospital blaze than she's telling him, and he's determined to get the truth—even if it means challenging her to face her tragic past. Summer is about to get hotter with this scorching novel from terrific talent Debra Dixon.

Mary Kay McComas is at her delightful best in **GOT IT BAD**, LOVESWEPT #793. When Dr. Mack McKissack storms the fortress of Kurt Andropov's laboratory to discover what he might be concealing, she doesn't plan on staying any longer than she has to in the devil's lair! Then a shocking accident places her in isolation with the maverick genius, and Mack has to deal not only with the unknown bug that threatens their lives, but also with the fiery attraction arcing between two rivals on the edge. Mary Kay Mc-Comas delivers pure gold with this hilarious, outrageous, and heartwarming romance.

Happy reading!

With warmest wishes,

Beth de Guzman

Shauna Summers

Beth de Guzman

Senior Editor

Shauna Summers

Editor

P.S. Watch for these Bantam women's fiction titles coming in June: From Jane Feather—the incomparable author of national bestsellers VIOLET and VALENTINE—comes **VICE**, her newest unforgettable romance. Suzanne Robinson takes readers back to the Victorian world of LADY DANGEROUS in **THE ENGAGEMENT**, a mesmerizing love story about a freethinking young woman and a gun-toting Texan. Bestselling author Sandra Canfield, author of DARK JOURNEY, presents a gripping tale as a desperate call from the past throws a man and a woman together again in **NIGHT MOVES.** Finally, from Susan Johnson, the award-winning mistress of sizzling historical romance, comes **SWEET LOVE, SURVIVE,** the powerful conclusion to the bestselling Kuzan Dynasty series begun in SEIZED BY LOVE and LOVE STORM.

Be sure to see next month's LOVESWEPTs for a preview of these exceptional novels. And immediately following this page, preview the Bantam women's fiction titles on sale now!

Don't miss these extraordinary books
by your favorite Bantam authors

On sale in April:

THE UGLY DUCKLING
by Iris Johansen

THE UNLIKELY ANGEL
by Betina Krahn

DANGEROUS TO HOLD
by Elizabeth Thornton

THE REBEL AND THE REDCOAT
by Karyn Monk

New York Times bestselling author of *Lion's Bride*

IRIS JOHANSEN

creates a thrilling world of sinister intrigue and dark
desire in her spectacular contemporary hardcover
debut

THE UGLY
DUCKLING

"Crackling suspense and triumphant romance with a
brilliant roller coaster of a plot."   —Julie Garwood

*Plain, soft-spoken Nell Calder isn't the type of woman to
inspire envy, lust—or murderous passions. Until one night
on an exotic island in the Aegean Sea, at an elegant gathering that should have cemented her husband's glorious
career in finance, the unimaginable happens . . . and in
the space of a heartbeat, Nell's life, her dreams, her future
are shattered by a spray of bullets and the razor edge of a
blade. Though badly hurt, Nell emerges from the night-
mare a woman transformed. Delicate surgery gives her an
exquisitely beautiful face. Rehabilitation gives her a strong,
lithe body. And Nicholas Tanek, a mysterious stranger who
compels both fear and fascination, gives her a reason to go
on living: revenge—at any price.*

The information was wrong, Nicholas thought in disgust as he gazed down at the surf crashing on the
rocks below. No one would want to kill Nell Calder.

   If there was a target here, it was probably Kavinski. As head of an emerging Russian state he had the

power to be either a cash cow or extremely troublesome. Nell Calder wouldn't be considered troublesome to anyone. He had known the answers to all the questions he had asked her but he had wanted to see her reactions. He had been watching her all evening and it was clear she was a nice, shy woman, totally out of her depth even with those fairly innocuous sharks downstairs.

Unless she was more than she appeared. Possibly. She seemed as meek as a lamb but she'd had the guts to toss him out of her daughter's room when she had enough of him.

Still, everyone fought back if the battle was important enough. She hadn't wanted to share her daughter with him. No, the information must mean something else. When he went back downstairs he would stay close to Kavinski.

> "Here we go up, up, up
> High in the sky so blue.
> Here we go down, down, down
> Brushing the rose so red."

She was singing to the kid. He had always liked lullabies. There was a sense of warmth and reassurance about them that had been missing in his own life. Since the dawn of time mothers had sung to their children and they would probably still be singing to them a thousand years from now.

The song ended with a low chuckle and murmured words he couldn't hear.

Nell came out of the bedroom and closed the door a few minutes later. She was flushed and glowing with an expression as soft as melted butter.

"I've never heard that lullaby before," he said.

She looked startled, as if she'd forgotten he was still here. "It's very old. My grandmother used to sing it to me."

"Is Jill asleep?"

"No, but she will be soon. I started the music box for her again. By the time it finishes, she usually nods off."

"She's a beautiful child."

"Yes." A luminous smile turned her plain face radiant. "Yes, she is."

He stared at her, intrigued. He found he wanted to keep that smile on her face. "And bright?"

"Sometimes too bright. Her imagination can be troublesome. But she's always reasonable and you can talk to—" She broke off and her eagerness faded. "But this can't interest you. I forgot the tray. I'll go back for it."

"Don't bother. You'll disturb Jill. The maid can pick it up in the morning."

She gave him a level glance. "That's what I told you."

He smiled. "But then I didn't want to listen. Now it makes perfect sense to me."

"Because it's what you want to do."

"Exactly."

"I have to go back too. I haven't met Kavinski yet." She moved toward the door.

"Wait. I think you'll want to remove that smear of chocolate from the skirt of your gown first."

"Damn." She frowned as she looked down at the stain. "I forgot." She turned toward the bathroom and said dryly, "Go on. I assure you I don't need your help with this problem."

He hesitated.

She glanced at him pointedly over her shoulder.

He had no excuse for staying, not that that small fact would have deterred him.

But he also had no reason. He had been steered wrong. He had lived by his instincts too long not to trust them, and right now they were telling him this woman wasn't a target of any sort. He should be watching Kavinski.

He turned toward the door. "I'll tell the maid you're ready for her to come back."

"Thank you, that's very kind of you," she said automatically as she disappeared into the bathroom.

Good manners obviously instilled from childhood. Loyalty. Gentleness. A nice woman whose world was centered on that sweet kid. He had definitely drawn a blank.

The maid wasn't waiting in the hallway. He'd have to send up one of the servants from downstairs.

He moved quickly through the corridors and started down the staircase.

Shots.

Coming from the ballroom.

Christ.

He tore down the stairs.

She was too good to be true.
He was too bad to resist.

Experience the enchanting wit of
New York Times bestselling
BETINA KRAHN
author of *The Last Bachelor* and
The Perfect Mistress

in the delicious new love story
THE UNLIKELY ANGEL

With her soft heart and angelic face, Madeline Duncan is no one's idea of a hardheaded businesswoman. So when the lovely spinster comes into an unexpected inheritance and uses her newfound wealth to start a business, she causes quite a stir . . . especially with barrister Lord Cole Mandeville, who has been appointed by the courts to keep Madeline from frittering away her fortune. Handsome, worldly, and arrogant, Cole knows just how ruthless the world can be—and that an innocent like Miss Duncan is heading straight for heartbreak, bankruptcy, or worse. But when he sets out to show Madeline the error of her ways, Cole is in for the surprise of his life . . . as he finds himself falling under the spell of a woman who won't believe the worst about anyone—even a jaded rogue like him.

"One of the genre's most creative writers. Her
ingenious romances always entertain and leave
the readers with a warm glow."
—*Romantic Times*

Spellbinding. Intoxicating. Riveting.
Elizabeth Thornton's gift for romance is nothing
less than addictive. Now from this bestselling
author comes her most passionate love story yet.

DANGEROUS TO HOLD

by

ELIZABETH THORNTON

*He'd accosted her on a dark London street, sure that she
was his missing wife. But a few moments in her company
assured Marcus Lytton that Miss Catherine Courtnay was
nothing like Catalina. Cool and remote, with a tongue as
tart as a lemon and eyes that could flash with temper, the
fiery-haired beauty was everything his scheming adventur-
ess wife wasn't—innocent, loyal, and honest. And so he
uttered the words that would sweep Catherine into his life,
and into a desperate plan that could spell disaster for them
both: "I want you to play the part of my wife. . . ."*

"You are, are you not, my lord, a *married* man?"

The smile was erased. "What do you know of my
wife?" he asked.

She hesitated, shrugged, and said boldly, "Until
tonight, I knew only what everyone else knows, that

you'd married a Spanish girl when you served with Wellington in Spain."

"And after tonight?"

This time she did not falter. "I know that you hate her enough to kill her."

His eyes burned into hers, then the look was gone and the careless smile was in place. "You have misread the situation. It is my wife who wishes to kill me. She may yet succeed. Oh, don't look so stricken. I believe it happens in the best of families. Divorce is so hard to come by, and for a Catholic girl the word doesn't exist." His voice turned hard. "So you see, Catalina and I are bound together until death us do part. An intolerable situation."

Her mind was racing off in every direction. There were a million questions she wanted to ask, but she dared not voice a single one. Even now he was suspicious of her. She could feel it in her bones.

She tried to look amused. "I'm sure, my lord, you are exaggerating."

"Am I? I wonder." His mood changed abruptly. "Enough about me. I am at a disadvantage here. I know nothing about you, and until I know more, I refuse to let you go."

He spoke gaily, as though it were all a great game, but she wasn't taken in by it. She'd seen that darker side of him and knew that the danger wasn't over yet. She intended, if at all possible, to leave this place without his knowing who she was or where to find her.

She moistened her lips. "My lord, I appeal to you as a gentleman to let me go. You see, there is someone waiting for me. If he were to hear of my . . . misadventure, it could prove awkward for me."

There was a strange undercurrent in the silence,

as though her words disturbed him in some way. "I see," he said. "And this gentleman, I take it, is someone you met tonight at Mrs. Spencer's house. Did you make a secret assignation?"

Alarm coursed through her veins. "Mrs. Spencer? I know no one by that name."

"Don't you? I could have sworn that I saw you leave her house tonight. What happened? Did you quarrel? Did she throw you out in those rags? I know how jealous women can be. And you are very beautiful. Did you steal one of her lovers? Is that it? Who is waiting for you? Is it Worcester? Berkeley? Whatever they offered, I can do better."

A moment before, she had been trembling in her shoes. Now a wave of rage flooded through her. Each question was more insulting than the last, and he was doing it on purpose. This time, when she rose to her feet, there was no tremor in her knees. She was Catherine Courtnay and no man spoke to her in those terms. "My business with Mrs. Spencer," she said, "is no concern of yours."

"So, you were there!"

"And if I was?"

There was a moment when she knew she had made that blunder she had tried so hard to avoid. He rose to face her and his eyes glittered brilliantly. Then he reached for her, and hard, muscular arms wrapped around her, dragging her against thighs of iron and a rock-hard chest. She could feel the brass buttons of his coat digging into her. Her arms were trapped at her sides. One hand cupped her neck, then his lips were against her mouth.

From the exciting new voice of

KARYN MONK

author of *Surrender to a Stranger*

THE REBEL AND THE REDCOAT

"Karyn Monk . . . brings the romance of the era to readers with her spellbinding storytelling talents. This is a new author to watch." —*Romantic Times*

When he saw the lovely young woman struggling with her captor, Damien didn't care which side of the bloody war she was on. He only knew that he had never seen such extraordinary beauty and raw courage in his life. Yet Damien couldn't know that one day this innocent farm girl was destined to betray him. She would become Charles Town's most irresistible spy, dazzling officers with her charms even as she stripped them of strategic secrets. But when a twist of fate brings Josephine back into his life again, Damien will gamble everything on the chance that he can make this exquisite rebel surrender . . . if only in his arms.

Jo stiffened with terror as she lay on the ground and waited for the Indian's blade to carve into her back. Despite her determination not to show her fear, a sob escaped her lips. She was going to die. She waited for her body to be ruthlessly stabbed. The Indian fell heavily onto her, crushing her with his weight, and she screamed, a scream born of utter despair. She had failed. Now Anne and Lucy and Samuel would die. The warrior jerked a few times. Then he let out a sigh and was still. Jo lay frozen beneath him, uncertain what had happened.

Damien dropped his pistol and collapsed against the ground, cursing with every breath he took. He realized his wound was severe, and that he was losing a tremendous amount of blood. He rolled onto his back and vainly tried to stanch the flow with his hands. In a moment or two he would be so weak he would be past the point of caring whether or not he bled to death. It was strange, he mused grimly, but somehow when he had come to the colonies he had not imagined his death would be at the hands of an Indian as he tried to save a simple farm girl.

"Are you all right, Jo?" demanded Samuel anxiously. He moved to where she lay buried beneath the dead warrior.

"I think so," she managed, her voice thin and trembling. "Help me get him off."

Samuel grabbed one of the Indian's arms and pulled. Jo pushed until the dead man's body moved enough for her to scramble out from underneath it. The minute she was free she rushed over to the injured man who had saved her life.

Her throat constricted in horror as she stared down at him. Numbly she took in the scarlet color of his torn jacket, the white waistcoat stained ruby with blood, and the filthy white of his breeches. "Oh dear Lord," she gasped, appalled. "You're a *redcoat*!"

Damien forced his eyes open to look at the woman who had cost him his life. Her eyes were the color of the sky, as clear and brilliant a shade of blue as he had ever seen. Her sunlit hair tumbled wildly over her shoulders, forming a golden veil of silk around her. *It was worth it*, he decided absently as pain clouded over his mind.

She did not move closer but continued to stare at him, her expression a mixture of wariness and fear. He frowned, wondering why she was afraid. And then her words pierced through the dark haze that had almost claimed his consciousness.

Christ, he thought as blackness drowned his senses.

A bloody patriot.

To enter the sweepstakes outlined below, you must respond by the date specified and follow all entry instructions published elsewhere in this offer.

DREAM COME TRUE SWEEPSTAKES

Sweepstakes begins 9/1/94, ends 1/15/96. To qualify for the Early Bird Prize, entry must be received by the date specified elsewhere in this offer. Winners will be selected in random drawings on 2/29/96 by an independent judging organization whose decisions are final. Early Bird winner will be selected in a separate drawing from among all qualifying entries.

Odds of winning determined by total number of entries received. Distribution not to exceed 300 million.

Estimated maximum retail value of prizes: Grand (1) $25,000 (cash alternative $20,000); First (1) $2,000; Second (1) $750; Third (50) $75; Fourth (1,000) $50; Early Bird (1) $5,000. Total prize value: $86,500.

Automobile and travel trailer must be picked up at a local dealer; all other merchandise prizes will be shipped to winners. Awarding of any prize to a minor will require written permission of parent/guardian. If a trip prize is won by a minor, s/he must be accompanied by parent/legal guardian. Trip prizes subject to availability and must be completed within 12 months of date awarded. Blackout dates may apply. Early Bird trip is on a space available basis and does not include port charges, gratuities, optional shore excursions and onboard personal purchases. Prizes are not transferable or redeemable for cash except as specified. No substitution for prizes except as necessary due to unavailability. Travel trailer and/or automobile license and registration fees are winners' responsibility as are any other incidental expenses not specified herein.

Early Bird Prize may not be offered in some presentations of this sweepstakes. Grand through third prize winners will have the option of selecting any prize offered at level won. All prizes will be awarded. Drawing will be held at 204 Center Square Road, Bridgeport, NJ 08014. Winners need not be present. For winners list (available in June, 1996), send a self-addressed, stamped envelope by 1/15/96 to: Dream Come True Winners, P.O. Box 572, Gibbstown, NJ 08027.

THE FOLLOWING APPLIES TO THE SWEEPSTAKES ABOVE:

No purchase necessary. No photocopied or mechanically reproduced entries will be accepted. Not responsible for lost, late, misdirected, damaged, incomplete, illegible, or postage-die mail. Entries become the property of sponsors and will not be returned.

Winner(s) will be notified by mail. Winner(s) may be required to sign and return an affidavit of eligibility/release within 14 days of date on notification or an alternate may be selected. Except where prohibited by law, entry constitutes permission to use of winners' names, hometowns, and likenesses for publicity without additional compensation. Void where prohibited or restricted. All federal, state, provincial, and local laws and regulations apply.

All prize values are in U.S. currency. Presentation of prizes may vary; values at a given prize level will be approximately the same. All taxes are winners' responsibility.

Canadian residents, in order to win, must first correctly answer a time-limited skill testing question administered by mail. Any litigation regarding the conduct and awarding of a prize in this publicity contest by a resident of the province of Quebec may be submitted to the Regie des loteries et courses du Quebec.

Sweepstakes is open to legal residents of the U.S., Canada, and Europe (in those areas where made available) who have received this offer.

Sweepstakes in sponsored by Ventura Associates, 1211 Avenue of the Americas, New York, NY 10036 and presented by independent businesses. Employees of these, their advertising agencies and promotional companies involved in this promotion, and their immediate families, agents, successors, and assignees shall be ineligible to participate in the promotion and shall not be eligible for any prizes covered herein. SWP 3/95